Blanche Roosevelt, Blanche Roosevelt Tucker-Macchetta

The Home Life of Henry W. Longfellow

Reminiscences of many Visits at Cambridge and Nahant, during the years 1880,

1881 and 1882

Blanche Roosevelt, Blanche Roosevelt Tucker-Macchetta

The Home Life of Henry W. Longfellow
Reminiscences of many Visits at Cambridge and Nahant, during the years 1880, 1881 and 1882

ISBN/EAN: 9783337053826

Printed in Europe, USA, Canada, Australia, Japan

Cover: Foto ©Raphael Reischuk / pixelio.de

More available books at **www.hansebooks.com**

LONGFELLOW IN HIS STUDY AT CAMBRIDGE.

Cambs. March 14.

1882,

Dear Pandora,

Your telegram from
Washington brought me
your good wishes on my
birthday, and gave me
the greatest pleasure.

And now your
letter from New York
adds to that pleasure
and assures me that
amid your many oc-

cupations you have
time to remember me

You must not
think I am much troubled
by what the newspapers
say. I only wish they
would get things right.
It seems to me more
proper for me to know
nothing of the book,
beforehand, except
so far as matters of
fact are concerned.

But we will talk
of this more fully, when
I have the pleasure
of seeing you, which
I hope may be soon.

When you write to
Sr. Fontana I beg
you to thank him for
the copy of "Monte
Carlo", and also for
his kind intention of
sending me his poems

I am sorry I can
not say I am quite
well again. That would
be a poetic licence;
for I am still weak
and suffering

With best regards
to your husband, I
am as ever

Sincerely Yours
Ed. M. S.

THE HOME LIFE

OF

HENRY W. LONGFELLOW.

REMINISCENCES

OF

MANY VISITS AT CAMBRIDGE AND NAHANT,

DURING THE YEARS 1880, 1881 AND 1882.

BY

BLANCHE ROOSEVELT TUCKER-MACCHETTA.

NEW YORK:

Copyright, 1882, by

G. W. Carleton & Co., Publishers.

LONDON: S. LOW, SON & CO.

MDCCCLXXXII.

Stereotyped by
SAMUEL STODDER,
ELECTROTYPER & STEREOTYPER,
90 ANN STREET, N. Y.

TROW
PRINTING AND BOOK-BINDING CO.
N. Y.

Dedication.

TO GEORGE I. SENEY,

A TRUE FRIEND, AND WISE COUNSELOR,

THIS, MY FIRST WORK,

IS AFFECTIONATELY DEDICATED,

IN WARM AND GRATEFUL REMEMBRANCE.

INTRODUCTION.

DURING the month of July, 1880, I had the pleasure of spending several days at Nahant, as the guest of Henry W. Longfellow, and at his suggestion, I kept the journal from which these pages have been taken.

Honored with the poet's friendship, I could not but appreciate the benefit of passing much time in his society, and seeing him in the home circle, where the genuineness of his nature could best be understood. For nearly three years I had been in active correspondence with him. My friends expressed so much curiosity regarding the home life of so great a man that the idea came to me to make use of my journal and publish a book of Reminiscences. Having thought long and seriously on the subject I prepared more than half of the present work, and on the twenty-eighth of last December, in response to the following letter, I went with my sister to Cambridge, where we spent the day with the poet:

"CAMBRIDGE, *December* 27*th*, 1881.

"DEAR PANDORA:*—I have just received your telegram and am so glad you are coming, and so sorry that I cannot come in to welcome you. Alas! I am still confined to the house, and mostly to my room.

"Please come and see me to-morrow forenoon at eleven, if possible; not in the afternoon, as I have to sleep.

"How delightful it will be to see you again. I wish I could give a better account of myself. I improve very, *very* slowly.

        "Yours faithfully,

           "H. W. LONGFELLOW."

Mr. Longfellow expressed himself as very much pleased with my idea and what I had done. He said we would call the work "Reminiscences of a Poet's

---

* "Pandora" was the title with which the Poet usually addressed me.

Home Life." He corrected with his own hand many lines, and made many suggestions. I wrote them down in full. He reviewed and revised all that was written most thoroughly, and remarked on the chapter containing his personal description : " Why, that is my portrait ; flattered certainly, but it *is* me, and I will never have another taken better than that."

He rather objected to the description of his visit to Queen Victoria, but finally withdrew his opposition. It would have been a pity to overlook so salient a point in his character of an American poet. It was decided that I should bring him the manuscript (the last six chapters were only sketched out) in its entirety, when he would make necessary corrections, and revise it completely.

His sudden demise hastened the appearance of this little work. My husband and myself dined with Mr. T. G. Appleton the evening of March 28th. I then read to him the entire work, receiving at the time many newer suggestions and several important facts from the poet's brother-in-law, which are here incorporated.

My thanks are tendered to Mr. T. G. and Mr. Nathan Appleton for their kindly interest and suggestions, and to Miss Fannie A. Tucker.

The book pretends to claim no literary merit ; it
is merely an humble and affectionate tribute, not
alone to the great poet, but to the cherished friend.

BLANCHE ROOSEVELT MACCHETTA.

NEW YORK, *April*, 1882.

CONTENTS.

CHAPTER I.—*Cambridge.—The Home of the Poet, II. W. Longfellow.—Entrance to his House.— Longfellow follows the Custom of the Ancients. — Reception by the Poet.—Introduction to the famous Study.—The beauty of the House.— The Craigie Mansion, once Washington's Head-quarters.—Lady Washington's Room. — The Portraits.—Tintoretto and David.—A Re-markable Fire-place.—An Old Clock on the Stairs.—Luncheon, and Longfellow's Remarks on Jules Janin* 19

CHAPTER II.—*A second Visit to Cambridge.—De-scription of the Poet.—Longfellow as he appears at Seventy-four* 43

CHAPTER III.—*The Promenade on the Terrace.— Longfellow will call Things by their Right*

[15]

*Names.—Living in a —— Yellow House.—
Visitors, and his Reception of them.—An Au-
tograph for a Namesake.—His last Visit to
England.—His Call on Her Majesty Queen
Victoria.—The Difference in Poets.—Long-
fellow a Poet of the People.—The Queen's
Remark, "Why, even all my Servants read
your Poems."—The real Dante.—Sketch of the
Italian Poet.—A rare Autograph Album* . 48

CHAPTER IV.—*Nahant. — The Poet's Summer
Home.—How he spends his Mornings.—Modest
Interior of the Poet's House.—A well-bred Gentleman living in quiet Luxury.—His Habits
and Correspondence.—His Love of Fun* . 65

CHAPTER V.—*A morning Occupation.—The Professor an early Riser.—The Ceremony used by
the Family towards each other.—A Family
Party at Table, and General Conversation on
the Terrace.—The Poet's Letters.—His Handwriting.—Accidental Discovery of a New
Author.—Unearthing of a Poet.—Rubbish,
and my Unfortunate Remark.—Description of
the Poet's Laugh* 80

CHAPTER VI.—*Longfellow Speaks of Poetical Influence.—The Works he never Reads.—Sketch
and his Opinion of Alfred de Musset, the French
Poet.—"A God-given Talent put to bad Uses."
—Longfellow not Willing to lie awake at Night*

to set a bad Example to a Class of thirty the
next Morning 95

CHAPTER VII.—*The Poet's Appreciation of Paro-
dies.—A Household Word.—"I know the
Lines."—Dante in another Form.—An English
Parody on Hiawatha* 108

CHAPTER VIII.—*Longfellow visits Jules Janin, the
French Critic.—The Impression made on his
Mind by his Mode of Living.—In Doubt as
to an old Acquaintance.—Byron and Swinburne* 119

CHAPTER IX.—*Longfellow with his Grandchild.—
Youth and Old Age.—Sketch of the Late Victor
Emmanuel, King of Italy.—The Poet's Greet-
ing to his Family* 130

CHAPTER X.—*A Drive to Lynn.—Mr. Longfellow's
Love of the Sea.—Where he Wrote his Poems
"A Secret of the Sea" and "Palingenesis."—
The Real Story of Hyperion* 142

CHAPTER XI.—*Longfellow's Love of Flowers.—The
Pink Pond Lily.—A Poetic Sketch.—An
Honest Opinion* 155

CHAPTER XII.—*Longfellow in Conversation.—A
Good Listener.—Characteristic Habits.—The
Golden Century.—The Glory of the Nine-
teenth* 165

Chapter XIII.—*A Wedding Anniversary.—The Real Way to made Fish Chowder.—Poem, " The Bells of Lynn"* 174

Chapter XIV.—*The Evening at Nahant.—Longfellow's Love of Music.—Fond of Rossini. —Recitation of a Favorite Poem by the Poet* 183

Chapter XV.—*Talk on Poets.—Sketch, Victor Hugo.—Longfellow Wishes to Shake him by the Hand* 193

Chapter XVI.—*Visit to Cambridge a Year later. —Christmas Dinner in the Craigie Mansion.— Tales of a Wayside Inn.—All Characters from Life.—Portrait of The Sicilian, Luigi Monti* 210

Chapter XVII.—*My Lost Youth.—Pen Portrait of G. W. Greene.—The Historian and Longfellow.—Friends of over Three-score Years.— The Study at Cambridge, in the Lamplight. —Mr. Longfellow Speaks of Edgar Allan Poe* 221

Chapter XVIII.—*Looking over my Journal.—My last visit to Cambridge.—The Poet Ill and Suffering.—Hoping for another May* . . 237

Chapter XIX.—*Ultima Thule.—The last Resting-place of the great Poet* 245

LONGFELLOW'S HOME LIFE.

——•◦•——

CHAPTER I.

THE HOUSE AT CAMBRIDGE.

"Once, ah ! once within these walls,
One, whom memory oft recalls,
The Father of his Country, dwelt."

To a Child.

"MY Dear Madam :—I have arranged it all, and will call for you to-morrow at eleven. Excuse my coming so early, but it is a long way to Cambridge, and luncheon is usually at one o'clock. The Poet says he will be charmed to see you. In haste.

"Votre dévoué,
"Nathan Appleton."

Such is the substance of a little note that I am continually turning over and over in my hand. As

I read and re-read it I know that a great desire of
my life is on the eve of realization. I am going
to Cambridge. Cambridge is the home of a poet,
and that poet is Henry Wadsworth Longfellow.

When I was in Paris, in the Spring of '79, I
made the acquaintance of Mr. Nathan Appleton,
our distinguished compatriot, who had come to
Europe as a delegate to the International Congress,
called together by Count Ferdinand de Lesseps,
regarding a maritime canal across the American
isthmus.　Mr. Appleton is a brother-in-law of
Mr. Longfellow, and he had promised to present
me to the poet if ever I should go to Boston. I
am here now, and this little note is the agreeable
result.

The hours passed slowly till the following morning, and only as we drove through the well-kept
carriage-way did I feel that my time of probation
was ended. Ascending the old-fashioned steps, we
found ourselves on the porch of the Craigie Mansion.
We walked towards the entrance, and to my amaze-

ment Mr. Appleton did not ring, but turned the knob softly, saying,

"Longfellow follows the custom of the ancients. His latch-string is ever out." Or, I interrupted,

"The peasants of Normandy in the reign of the Henrys. 'Neither locks had they to their doors, nor bars to their windows; but their dwellings were open as day and the hearts of the owners.'"

We entered a large antechamber which reminded me of the small chamber in the Louvre of Paris, dedicated to the Venus of Milo, and, in fact, almost the first object my eye rested upon was a copy of that wondrous work. The walls were hung with plaques and pictures, while copies and originals in ancient sculpture were artistically placed about. In one corner, on a high pedestal, was a beautiful head in white marble of the Roman hero Marcellus—a copy of the famous bust in the antique museum in Rome; it is so well done as to almost rival in beauty the great original.

There were several doors to this apartment, and one at the farther end stood open. A maid came forward, and Mr. Appleton, recognizing her with a smile, inquired if the poet were visible. She answered in the affirmative, and showed the way through a richly-furnished hall to his study. As our advancing footsteps made themselves heard the door opened and Longfellow stood before us.

With well-bred civility, he acknowledged Mr. Appleton's introduction, and his first words were calculated to set me at my ease. The apartment in which we found ourselves was very large, and a huge open fire-place occupied considerable space at the left of the entrance. The morning was chilly, and a soft fire of cannel coal intermingled with logs of hickory shot a cheerful glow up into the wide chimney.

While the poet was engaged with Mr. Appleton, I looked around and examined the apartment at my fullest leisure. I lost no time in concluding that I was in the famous study of the poet, and what a study!

The room, about thirty feet square, seemed of more ample dimensions. There was a harmonious blending of furniture, walls, books, pictures and statuary. The prevailing tint a warm Autumn brown—a sympathetic golden that comes to the leaves in October, when, fanned by the western winds, they deepen in color as they catch the glow of a fading Summer's sun.

The day was so misty without that it threw in bold relief the exquisite warmth and comfort within. A fire-light cast fitful gleams of brightness on the russet brown of the carpet, and dimly illumined even the furthermost objects in the apartment. I was absolutely penetrated with the atmosphere of repose and poetry of this wondrous chamber. My lips moved involuntarily, and I spoke rather than thought the word,

" *Simpatica.*" The poet's voice interrupted my revery.

" I see that you are pleased with my study, and have divined the very name that my heart so long has given it. Besides being comfortable, there is one capital reason why it should be called sympathetic. This was Washington's own private room ; and where my writing-desk now stands, there stood his table. These walls, lined with books, also shelved his literary lore. In fact, I think the arrangement of the room is exactly the same as when in his time."

I looked around and said, musingly :

> " Once, ah ! once within these walls,
>   One, whom memory oft recalls,
>   The Father of his Country, dwelt."

Thrilled with the influence of the past, I almost expected to see the desk piled with maps and charts, and the paraphernalia of a General's budget. Instead, on either side of a carved portfolio was a mass of letters; those on the left with faces downward were answered (so the poet explained), those on the right, turned upwards, awaited his convenience for a response. A beautiful ink-stand attracted my attention.

"It belonged to Coleridge," said Longfellow, simply.

" And the quills ?" 1 asked, referring to a package lying beside it.

" Belong to me," added the poet, with a cunning smile.

" I see," said I, laughing lightly, "you think, with the Earl of Dudley, that it is beneath the dignity of a gentleman to write with anything but a quill. I was once guilty of answering an invitation in a way that called this comment down on my head. His lordship explained further, that in the best circles of England it is considered positively a breach of etiquette to send a letter written with a steel pen."

It was impossible in looking around the room not to notice the many rare objects that adorned it. The bookcases were Parisian and magnificently carved; all that is valuable in ancient and modern literature peeped out from behind the glass, and in one was a still rarer treasure—the original manuscript of all the poet's own works. On a beautiful table between the windows reposed an immense volume which the poet took up lovingly. It was a copy of the Lord's Prayer, printed in every known language ; a most valuable work and an exquisite testimonial of the book-binder's art.

The walls were hung with perfect likenesses in crayon of Emerson, Nathaniel Hawthorne, Charles Sumner and Felton; and near the door an excellent likeness of the poet himself, although taken many years ago. Opposite his desk was a bust of General Green's grandson, G. W. Green, capable historian and Longfellow's dear friend. Over the door nearest the window were two portraits, ancient, yellow and time-stained, but inestimable in value. One was George Washington, and the other, Martha, his wife. An orange-tree stood in one window; in the other a high desk where the poet used often to write standing, and by the fireside was the already famous children's chair. The center-table was carelessly laden with choice volumes. I picked up one and read "The Scarlet Letter."

"What a wonderful book," I exclaimed.

"Yes, in truth a wonderful book," responded Longfellow, "I have read it many times, and think it stands pre-eminent among works of American fiction.

Hawthorne was my dear friend, yet I speak without prejudice."

I had thought that this room held all that was valuable in literature, but the professor laughingly opened a door to the right, disclosing a small room, absolutely filled with books, pamphlets and papers. Here are hidden some of his most valuable works; among them some original Bodonis, which marked the first great era in the art of Italian printing. This is also the legitimate home of the copy of the Lord's Prayer which was on the table by accident that day.

From the study we passed into Lady Washington's parlor, which now serves as a morning-room. An immense oil painting representing the children of Sir William Pepperill, the old colonial governor, the figures dressed in the fashion of his time, lent an added charm of quaintness to the apartment. The old-fashioned simplicity of the furniture in its stately repose seemed almost to bespeak the presence of the "First lady in the Land" as she was then called, and even a quantity of modern bric-a-brac could not entirely dispel the idea.

We stopped in an adjoining antechamber to admire two marvelous works of art—one a David, his own picture painted by himself, the other a Tintoretto, the head of a Venetian soldier. To one familiar with the many originals in the galleries of Venice, it was easy to recognize in the present picture one of the painter's master-pieces. Longfellow looked long and earnestly at both works, and pointed out with the eye of a connoisseur the salient points, the perfection of each as a work of art, yet withal the astonishing difference in the school of painting. Then ensued a discussion on the two artists and their works.

Tintoretto seems to have shown, in very early youth, a decided talent for painting. He first commenced decorating the walls of the house, and all the surrounding objects about the paternal workshop were covered with bold drawings of heads and faces. His good father, although only a poor dyer, determined, at last, to give the lad the best education that his means would permit. Some say he was born in 1512, others in 1517, and one may as well

accept the last statement as the first. He certainly
was born about that time, and his real name was
Robusti—Jacobo Robusti, a solid Italian cognomen,
and the one that decorated the gilded sign over his
father's workshop in far-famed Venice—already
the birth-place of many great men, not alone among
whom was Tiziano, Morone and Bonifazio. To this
list of artists we certainly may add "little Tintoretto," as he was called, because of his father being
a dyer. "Tintura" is the Italian for "color," and
"tintore" naturally is for that of a "colorer;"
hence "tintoretto" is the diminutive for "little
dyer." He was so clever that his pictures were
often painted without being drawn, although, when
he reached man's estate, he showed his appreciation
of the art of drawing by taking Michel Angelo for
his guide. Tiziano, his master, figured side by side
with the great sculptor as pre-eminent in the art of
coloring; in fact, the motto over his door was "*Il
disegno di Michel Angelo il colorito di Tiziano.*"
("The drawing of Michel Angelo and the coloring of
Tiziano.") It is said that his best pieces are "The

Passion of our Savior," and the "Miracle of St. Marc." He painted so fast and with such profusion that his may be claimed as the most prolific of all Italian pencils. His works were all good, if not great. He was especially happy in portraits, and here we find the great precepts learned of his master, Tiziano, carried out with extraordinary vigor and fidelity. Seeing only the large pictures he has done one might well consider him a wonder, but on examining those of less pretense, one sees the same strength of color and a perfection of design worthy of Michel Angelo himself.

"This one," said the professor, looking straight at it, "merits more than a passing glance. See the deep, earnest eyes, delicate yet boldly traced lineaments and rich coloring. It seems impossible to realize that more than four centuries have elapsed since Tintoretto first put this face on canvas. It is distinct as if painted only a year ago, yet mellowed enough in tone by age to have watched with the night stars in Bethlehem when shepherds were awaiting the dawn."

"Well," said I, "I do not wonder that the son of the poor dyer caused his rivals many a sleepless night. His influence to-day, after four hundred years, alternately exalts and drives to despair the most ambitious and talented of his followers; yet with all his faults, the world would gladly give birth to another Tintoretto. It seems to me that when one has done so much that is great, history should kindly overlook the faults when they are in such minority."

"Oh, you may well say with all his faults," said Longfellow, laughingly, "poor Tintoretto has received unstinted praise and unstinted blame from historians of every century. Still, all seem to agree that he was incapable of real study. He abused a natural talent by drawing upon it at the last moment for work that another would have already prepared by faithful research and elaborate sketches. Strange to say, the more exorbitant the demand he made upon himself, and the more unreasonable, the more stupendous was the picture in an artistic sense. Perhaps, had he studied arduously, his works might all have been of equal excellence, and compatible with genius, which Macaulay defines as an 'infinite capacity for taking pains.'"

"Or according to this," I interrupted, "Tintoretto might have labored like a galley-slave, and yet left to the world no more mementos than the few that made his fame and are scattered here and there with a rarity which accords with their great excellence. Let us be content with little."

Tintoretto died in 1588. Nature denied him lineal descendants, but bestowed upon him the greater gift of living himself forever.

"Now," said the poet, "will you look at my David? The Tintoretto is wonderfully soft, but I must say I like the great character expressed in this face. David, you know, was a celebrated French painter of the last century, and while a man of great talent, there can be no comparison between himself and Tintoretto from an artistic standpoint. In the strength of character painting, however, they certainly had points in common. Look at this head, for instance. A great number of his pictures are in the gallery at Versailles, and some famous ones in the collection of the Luxembourg, in Paris. One of his finest works, "*La mort de la reine Elizabeth*," in the last-named place, is universally admired. The virgin queen is pictured half-raised from the pillow, endeavoring to have speech with her attendants, when she is stricken by the great destroyer. The terror and agony depicted on the countenance are so natural as to be alarming; the hard face of the queen, while retaining all of its usual characteristerics, wears also a new expression of humility that lessens the general repulsiveness and reflects wonderful credit on the able pencil of the painter. It is marvelous how, even in imagination, he could catch so fleeting an expression and so faithfully reproduce it."

"I remember well the picture always possessed a certain fascination for me," I answered, "and I think with you that David excels in portraits. As a colorist, he is crude and imitative, and his drawing never put Michel Angelo to the blush. He was really a sensational painter, and made stirring battle-pieces

2*

enough to satisfy the blood-thirsty in every land. The galleries in Versailles are filled with them. All of his works, however, have the quality of being intensely realistic. One might say that he has used miles of canvas, and his attempts were usually grandiose or very modest. There seemed little halfway work about him. He was a man of indefatigable energy, and while no one ever called him a genius, he will always be classed among the distinguished painters who have done great honor to France."

Leaving the antechamber we came to another room, corresponding in size to those previously seen. A substantial *buffet* in beautifully-carved wood suggested the nature of the apartment. Over it hung the portrait of Mr. T. G. Appleton, the poet's brother-in-law, taken in the Byronian style, at about the age of five-and-twenty. It was a fine face, and must have been an exceedingly good likeness.

Over the mantelpiece was a Roman picture by Guerra, in the style of the Mantegna frescoes. It was bought in the Piazzi di Spagna, in Rome, by Mr. Longfellow, and represents " A Cardinal and his suite on the Pincio." His Holiness is just stopping to admire the wonderful fountain so well known to all visitors to the Eternal City.

On one side of the room hung a portrait of three children, painted for the father, by Buchanan Read. All the world is familiar, if not with the painting, at least with its copies. A look of infinite tenderness came into the poet's face as we drew near to examine the picture, and he said, softly:

" Yes, those are my three little girls."

Mr. Appleton interrupted :

> " ' Grave Alice, laughing Allegra,
> And Edith, with golden hair.'

The one to the left is Edith, Mrs. Dana, the one to the right is the eldest daughter, Alice, and in the center is our little Annie."

While we were yet speaking Miss Annie came in. She greeted her father affectionately, and in a sweetly-modulated voice bade me welcome. The innate refinement of her manner was shown in the

ease with which she joined us. The poet then led
the way to the state parlor or drawing-room.

This room served formerly as a sort of council-
chamber for Washington and his staff.   It was
double the size of any chamber I had yet seen, re-
minding me, in its stateliness and beauty, of the East
Room of the White House.   Two ancient fluted pillars support the ceiling and form a natural panel in
the solid wall on one side.   At one end two windows
opened on a French terrace, while directly facing the
other was the glory of the apartment, a mammoth
fire-place.   Although not so antique, it has a striking
resemblance to the one in the house of William the
Conqueror at Dives, in Normandy. The old pile, at
present, is used as a tavern, but in one room the
grand old fire-place still remains in perfect preservation. We can readily imagine how Guillaume and
his bride, Mathilde of Flanders, sat together, as lovers
might, before their own hearth, and in remembrance
of the hour, scratched, in a stone in the chimney, the
letters G. and M., a souvenir that centuries has not
effaced.

Dives is not generally known to tourists, although it is not far from Paris. It would be insignificant, were it not for a certain Norman prettiness in the old houses.

" Thatched were the roofs, with dormer windows and gables projecting."

The gardens are quaint, and the actual existence of the home dwelt in by the Conqueror makes the spot interesting.

Pointing to the fire-place before us, the poet said, " This chimney is old, but the one up-stairs bears a plaque dated 1759."

We continued our examination of the apartment, but it would be impossible to describe all the costly and rare articles of vertu that adorned it. To the left of the fire-place stood a large Japanese folding screen, which partially hid a wall of books. I say " wall," as the cases seemed literally built in the side of the house. Opposite the columns was another large window, looking out on a side terrace, and commanding a beautiful view of the spacious grounds belonging to the place. In the window was a small writing-desk, furnished with other quills, trinkets ancient and modern, and a substantially well-filled portfolio. I took up a curious paper knife, which proved to be a dagger bearing the arms of Francis I., with the inscription " *Tout est perdu fors l'honneur.*"

Seated beside the poet, I followed with eager interest his gracious observations ; I think everything in the room received an affectionate tribute, and it was easy to see that every souvenir was held in constant remembrance by him.

The hands of many givers are peacefully folded to rest, while others still do their daily work in this busy life of ours.

A portrait of the Abbé Listz in his ecclesiastic gown, holding in his hand a flaring taper, was a striking likeness of the world-renowned pianist.

Admiring and discussing the time passed swiftly until we were summoned to luncheon. A cozy party sat down at table, and the poet made the tea. Honored with a place at his right, I was near enough to enjoy every word that fell from his lips. His conversation, spiced with admirable and appropriate wit, often sent the laugh around the festive board. He ate sparingly, yet with such intention, that no one could feel less frugal than he, verifying the difference between "living to eat, and—eating to live."

He enjoyed his tea, and I remarked on its flavor and color; a rich golden brown, it distilled an aroma particularly appetizing.

"I am glad you like it," said the poet heartily, "my son Charles brought it all the way from China."

Amongst other dishes, "*homard à la gelée*," excited the following remark from our host:

"I never see this dish without thinking of Jules Janin; in his remarks on fish, he called the lobster '*le cardinal de la mer*' (the cardinal of the sea); and we all know," with a deliciously sly laugh and a mirth-enlivened countenance, "that the lobster is not red until it has been boiled."

Adjoining to the drawing-room we lingered over our coffee, the conversation becoming ever more animated and brilliant until daylight gradually faded. Still under the charm of the professor's manner, a realizing sense of etiquette forced me to think of leaving. I arose hastily, pleading as an excuse for our long visit, that the poet himself had beguiled the hours away.

"It is a long distance to come," he said amiably, "and I thought this morning that it would be a dull day; but your visit has dispelled the clouds. Nathan," turning to Mr. Appleton, " you must persuade Madam to come again; you know *' les amis de mes amis sont mes amis.'* (The friends of my friends are my friends.)"

We retraversed the long hall and found ourselves in the front corridor. In turning to take a last look my eye rested on a wondrous time-piece, greatly resembling the one immortal in the poem, " The old clock on the stairs."

A broad staircase, with two landings, leads to the upper chambers. From the ceiling, resting on the first, stands this ancient time-piece. It is a magnificently carved Dutch clock with chimes, and is altogether a wonderful piece of mechanism. The long pendulum moved with a stately precision, and the tick,

tick, tick, was in agreeable and continuous harmony. The——but stop! Who would dare attempt a description of a clock with the poet's own loving portrayal of one before us.

> " Half-way up the stair it stands,
>   It points and beacons with its hands
>   From its case of massive oak,
>   Like a monk, who, under his cloak,
>   Crosses himself, and sighs, alas!
>   With sorrowful voice to all who pass,—
>   ' Forever——never!
>   Never——forever!' "

With these words ringing in my ears, I turned to the poet and said,

"So this inspired the poem we all know so well."

"No," said Mr. Longfellow, hastily, "that is the general idea, but it is erroneous. The real 'old clock on the stairs' is in possession of my brother, Mr. T. G. Appleton. When I wrote about it, it was in the old Plunkett-Gold mansion, where we resided when in Pittsfield, Massachusetts."

"Yes, I remember," I said, "these lines explain—

> ' Somewhat back from the village street
>   Stands the old-fashioned country-seat;
>   Across its antique portico
>   Tall poplar trees their shadows throw;
>   And from its station in the hall
>   An ancient time-piece says to all,—
>   Forever ——never!
>   Never ——forever!'

"That description also applies to this house; it stands somewhat back from the village street, and this clock is stationed half-way up the stairs."

"That probably gave rise to the mistake, but I will show you the real clock the next time you come to my brother's," said Mr. Appleton.

We then made our adieux

CHAPTER II.

PERSONAL DESCRIPTION OF THE POET.

" Stalworth and stately in form was the man of seventy
winters;
Hearty and hale was he, an oak, that is covered with
snowflakes;
White as the snow were his locks, and his cheeks as
brown as the oak leaves."

EVANGELINE, PART I.

HINKING over the events of the day in
the quietude of my chamber, the recol-
lection was so vivid, that I fancied myself still in the presence of the poet.
Longfellow must, in youth, have been what the
world calls a handsome man. His was a beauty of
color rather than classic regularity of feature. He
had long, light curling hair, which fell upon his
shoulders in tangled and graceful confusion. His

eyes were cerulean blue, and his face glowed with animation; the flesh tint being conspicuously bright and beautiful.

He was born February 27th, 1807, and since then the years of nearly three-quarters of a century have swept onward in their unending course. The slender lad grew to sensitive youth, living more within himself than with the outer world, and undoubtedly this extraordinary mental introspection did much to characterize his personal appearance. I could see in the exact pictures of him, taken at twenty, forty, and the later years of his life, the same unvarying, lineal features. His face, filled with rugged lines, presents a contour of great firmness and intelligence. The nose is Roman rather than Greek, with the very slightest aquiline tendency. His eyes are clear, straightforward, almost proud, yet reassuring, rather deeply set, and shaded by heavy, overhanging brows. In moments of lofty and inspired speech they have an eagle look, and the orbs deepen and flash. Like the great bird of prey, they seem to soar off into endless space, grasping in the talons of the mental vision, things unattainable to less ambitious flight. With his moods they vary, and when calm, nothing could exceed the quietness of their expression. If sad, an infinite tenderness reposes in their depths, and if merry, they sparkle and bubble over with fun. In fact, before the poet speaks, these traitorous eyes have already betrayed his humor. I must not forget the greatest of all expressions—humility. To one whose soul and mind are given to divine thought, 'tis in the eye that this sentiment finds its natural outcome. And the world knows that Longfellow's faith is the crowning gem in a diadem of virtues. His face is not a mask but an open book—a positive index to his character. His forehead is high, prominent, and square at the temples; numberless fine lines are ingrained in its surface, and on either side, a slender, serpentine vein starts from the eyes, and mounting upwards loses itself beneath a mass of silvery white hair. I should scarcely call them the work of time, but rather the marks of an over-active intelligence, and they may have appeared to

others at thirty as plainly as they do to me to-day.
The cheek-bones are high, and near the jaw the
cheeks are slightly sunken. The mouth is the most
sensitive feature in the face. Its character is mobile,
even yielding, absolutely belying the outspoken
firmness of the other features. The lips are rather
full, sharply outlined, and faintly tinged with color;
they close softly, and are sometimes tremulous with
emotional speech. Longfellow might be coaxed but
never driven. The whole of the face glows with a
beautiful carnation more suggestive of youth than
old age. The lower part is completely hidden by
a wavy beard of snowy whiteness, which also half
conceals the slender throat. The hair, mingling with
this, sets the rosy face in an aureole of snow. The
chest is broad, not deep. With a supple and graceful
carriage, he is straight as an arrow, and has a nature
of extraordinary vigor.

The charm of a well-bred manner asserts itself
over every other personal attribute. Were Longfellow less Longfellow—were he less characteristic
of a poet than a peasant, his courteous affability and

rare grace of manner would still far outshine many who have only this dependence for their success in life. His disposition is kindliness and sweetness itself, sympathetic, and utterly void of the slightest touch of vanity.

Perhaps I have drawn on my imagination, still, I think not. The first lines of Hyperion come into my mind—Hyperion, the greatest poem in modern prose :

"In John Lyly's 'Endymion,' Sir Topas is made to say: 'Dost thou know what a poet is? Why, fool, a poet is as much as one should say—a poet!' And thou, reader, dost thou know what a hero is? Why, a hero is as much as one should say—a hero!"

According to this, any further description would be ambiguous. Longfellow is a poet, and—my hero.

CHAPTER III.

A VISIT TO QUEEN VICTORIA.

" Not of the howling dervishes of song,
    Who craze the brain with their delirious dance,
    Art thou, oh, sweet historian of the heart.
    Therefore to thee the laurel leaves belong,
    To thee our love and our allegiance,
    For thy allegiance to the poet's art."
                    WAPENTAKE.—To ALFRED TENNYSON.

" Thy sacred song is like the trump of doom,
    Yet in thy heart what human sympathies,
    As up the convent walls, in golden streaks,
    The ascending sunbeams mark the day's decrease;
    And, as he asks what there the stranger seeks,
    Thy voice along the cloister whispers ' Peace.' "
                                    To DANTE.

T an early date, I availed myself of Mr. Longfellow's invitation to visit him again. As I drew near the house my eyes were gladdened with a sight of the poet. He was slowly pacing up and down the long terrace.

[48]

Enveloped in an old-fashioned mantle, one end of which was thrown carelessly over his shoulder, with an Alpine hat of soft brown felt, he looked a very handsome man, and the living embodiment of one of Sir Walter Scott's cavaliers.

Apparently he was better than when I last saw him. The fresh spring air and bright sunshine lent a glow to his cheek and an unusual brightness to his eye. He greeted me cordially. As he was taking his usual morning exercise, I begged not to interrupt, and together we continued the promenade up and down the old elm-shaded avenue, and back again to the front piazza. For the first time I noticed the house and its situation.

It stands on the road to Mount Auburn, about half a mile from Harvard College, and commands a perfect view of the Charles River, making a silver S in the meadow. It is quiet, unostentatious, and —yellow.

In speaking of it, Mr. Appleton suggested that I might at least dignify it with the name of "*écru*," whereat the poet said gravely,

3

"Go on, I don't mind what you call it, only it is yellow, and I like things to have their proper names."

Thus, lightly conversing, we went within doors.

Scarcely were we seated when the visitors' bell announced callers. This time I was a looker-on, and watched the poet's reception of his guests with infinite interest.

In a general conversation, an unerring instinct guided his questions and replies. He is so quick a reader of character, that not one word fell on an unappreciative person. Betrayed into some warmth of feeling at a casual remark, he commenced what would have been a glowing description of something he had seen, but, glancing a second time at his visitor, he quietly dropped the thread of his remarks. He knows instantaneously by the questions put to him, the mental calibre of each and every interlocutor.

Of course, as many epistolary tramps visit him out of curiosity, as well-intentioned *littérateurs* who worship at the shrine of poetic art. It was delicious to see him quietly put down the former without their

being aware of it, and to remark with what astute-
ness he divined the tastes of the latter mentioned.
Evidently the old adage of casting pearls before
swine is not unknown to him.

A bright little lad was shown into the room. He
was very young, perhaps seven years of age, and held
in his hand a newly-bound volume. His manner
suggested foreign breeding, as he bowed with mariou-
nette-like gravity to every one present, and there
stood still as if at a loss how to proceed.

Longfellow looked up smilingly; his love of children was evident in the mildness of his speech.

"Good morning, my lad," said he. "Did you
wish to see me?"

The boy said hesitatingly, "Professor Longfellow?"

"Yes," responded the poet kindly, "what is it?
Come hither."

"This is my birthday," he said, "and I have come
to beg you to put your autograph in my new album.
Mother just gave it to me, and she said she thought
I might ask you."

"What is your name?" asked the poet.

He looked up shyly. " I am named for you," he said simply, "and my father works in the college."

The poet was touched, and the shadows in his face deepened into tender thoughtfulness. He took the book, and after a moment inscribed the words, " To my little namesake. In remembrance of Henry W. Longfellow." He then drew the lad towards him, affectionately patted his head, and kissed his cheek in sign of adieu, at the same time sending his thanks to the mother for her kind remembrance. The boy went proudly out with his book under his arm, and this circumstance hastened the departure of the other guests.

Some new reviews and magazines being on the table, Longfellow turned to Mr. Appleton, and selecting one from amongst them, showed it to him. It was an English publication, and contained a criticism on himself and his works. In it the author called Longfellow a " poet of the people."

I had thought him above caring what a newspaper said about him, still his annoyance was visible

in the forced indifference of his tone while reading
it, and a short laugh which now and then half-escaped
him. The words " poet of the people " evidently
amused him, and in a careless, half-indifferent way
he asked Mr. Appleton's explanation of them. Mr.
Appleton hesitated, but I felt the way out of it.

The English critic, with natural pride, in referring to Tennyson as the " poet of the educated
masses," and to Longfellow as the " poet of the
people " unconsciously paid the highest compliment
to the latter. With this thought in my mind, I ventured to say, with reasonable assurance :

" The truly inspired address all the world when
they speak to the heart. Rienzi, the last of the
Roman tribunes, was not only a great man, but a
poet of the people, and he said ' *Vox populi, vox
Dei.*' Blind Homer did not improvise for kings and
queens, yet the Iliad and Odyssey stand to-day.
Dante's Divine Comedy is addressed to the people ;
Tasso and the great Ariosto were the people's poets,
although the former was so much in love with
Leonora as to ardently desire alliance with a duke's

sister; and in our own time Victor Hugo exiled himself to be able to write for them."

The urbanity of our poet was quite restored; he looked up with an entirely changed expression, and said, lightly:

"Speaking of all those European poets reminds me of my last visit to England. Shall I tell you about it? Would you care to hear?"

Would we care to hear! I should *think* we would.

We drew our chairs side by side, and Longfellow began:

"When I last went to England I was pleased and honored to receive an invitation from the queen to pay a visit to Windsor Castle. A royal invitation is a command, and being in Her Majesty's dominions, I obeyed. Windsor is but a short distance by rail from London. The Thursday following my arrival I presented myself at the palace. My name being announced, the late Lady Augusta Stanley came forward and received me with considerable ceremony. Passing through numerous apartments of great richness and historic beauty, I was finally left in an oval gallery of still more striking magnificence. She left me, saying that she would announce my visit to Her Majesty.

"In an incredibly short space of time Lady Stanley returned, and said that her royal mistress would be graciously pleased to receive me. I was then conducted forth from the room, and we passed through several long corridors. To my amazement doors were opened and shut, numberless heads peeped out, surreptitiously drew back, and mysterious whisperings seemed to fill the royal apartment with indefinable murmurings. This caused me wonderment, and no slight discomfort. I was directly ushered into the Throne Room. An imposing lady in black, with flowing drapery, came quickly forward to greet me. It was Her Majesty, Queen Victoria. She extended her hand, and I offered to take it."

"What!" I interrupted, "did you not bend and offer to kiss it?"

"No," said he, timidly, "I was not then familiar or acquainted with court etiquette, as I am now.

She offered me her hand evidently to shake, and I shook it."

"Why," said I, "she is the most inexorably *exigeante* of all sovereigns. You must have horrified her."

"I presume I did," said he simply. "Now I think of it, she was disconcerted, I suppose for that reason, but she rallied graciously, and asked me about America and myself. She explained,

"'We speak of America first, because you are America's poet. Tennyson is ours.'

"'Tennyson is the world's poet, Madam,' said I, bowing gravely. She smiled in gratified acquiescence and continued,

"'You are very generous.'

Her Majesty was then pleased to converse on general topics, but persistently got back to the subject of myself. I felt she was piqued about something at first, and her last words were:

"'We shall not forget you,' adding, with a laugh, 'why, *even* all my servants read your poems!'"

The poet then glanced up, and with an almost

comical expression, and, as after reading the criticism, he said,

"What do you think she intended by it? I was nonplussed, and to-day, although many years have passed, I am undecided as to what Her Majesty's real meaning was."

"Well, dear master," said I, "judging from Her Majesty's appreciation of the truly beautiful in art and nature, I think her words were meant to convey a decided compliment. It was hard for her to acknowledge that the poems of a foreigner were household words for even the lowest of her subjects, when her own Poet Laureate does not always succeed in making himself understood by the masses for whom he writes."

The poet looked up and said:

"Speaking of poets, have you seen my picture of Dante? It was supposed, after his death, that a portrait of him existed in the Bargello Palace, in Florence. All efforts to discover it had been futile, when in tearing down the fresco in one of the apartments, the head was discovered, but alas! not

3*

in a perfect state. The check under the left eye was irremediably scarred. Happily, I possess a correct drawing of the original."

We then went to examine it. I was surprised at the sweetness and extreme delicateness of the features.

"The pictures of the present day," said Longfellow, "are all taken from another view of the face, representing a much older man with matured features and sharply elongated countenance. The head is covered with a monk's cowl; a part of the shoulders are discovered, and in his hand he carries an ascetic flower. There is a boyish expression about the lips of the Bargello picture, which lends a charm not seen in those of a later date, and even the nose is without the accustomed sharpness.

"Richard Henry Wild, of Georgia, the author of the charming lines on the Tampa rose,

"My life is like the rose that blooms, &c.,"

when in Florence, became convinced that there must be under the whitewash of the Bargello Palace, a portrait of Dante. He induced Mr. Kirkup, an English artist of considerable influence in Florence, to persuade the government to allow him to make a search for the picture. The room was explored nearly through its entire length, when their faith was rewarded by discovering the now well-known fresco of the youthful Dante. The great interest of the head is in the fact that it expresses the sweet boyish face of the poet, as yet unfurrowed by care or torn by the terrible conflicts of his later life. One is all youthful hope and trust, and the other bitter, almost saturnine, with life-long warfare. To use Mr. Longfellow's own words,

> " Such a fate as this was Dante's,
> By defeat and exile maddened."

Dante was born in Florence, Italy, in the year 1265, in the thirteenth century, or, as it is called nowadays the "*tre cento*"—famous in Italian lore as the century most productive of the great lights of her literature. It is asserted by Ugolini, a Florentine, that Dante's father was a certain Aldighiero di

Bellincione, and that the poet was born outside the
city gates in a house of poor aspect, and of very humble dimensions.   The real truth is, that no one ever
knew positively *who* his father was.   There have
been many conjectures, many statements, but one
and all are alike inaccurate.   Dante grew to youth
with many children about Florence, and had a very
good tutor in the person of a certain Brunetto Latini.
At an early age he was studious, gentle, and chival-
rous   He went into the army at twenty-four, and
fought for his country at Campaldino, a brave soldier
and a true patriot; but in 1300, under Charles de
Valois, he was suspected of siding with the enemy,
and with a faithful few was exiled.   Shortly from
Gorgonza, where they had joined their forces, they
attacked Florence, but with defeat the only result.
Dante went to Verona and begged aid of the Scaligeri,
a noble house who flourished in that century, and
whose palaces and monuments to-day are among the
ancient glories of Verona—but from their refusal he
lost heart momentarily.   Dante was a man of wondrous courage and patience, and he tried in every

way, even through the medium of Pope Leon III., to raise his country to a harmonious and beautiful state, but he was only laughed at.

He was married to Gemma di Donati and had seven children, but the love of his life was Beatrice Portinari, and this affection, most beautiful in the annals of platonic regard, colored his whole existence, and is the most prominent figure in the part of his poem called "Il Paradiso." Dante wrote in verse and in prose in Italian, called the Vulgar tongue, and in Latin. His great poem is divided into three parts, and is called "la Divina Commedia" (the Divine Comedy). The first part is "l' Inferno" (the Lower Regions). The second is "Il Purgatorio" (Purgatory), and the third is "Il Paradiso" (Paradise). Although living at a time when everything was corrupt, Dante had a due regard for decency, and was unflagging in his efforts to uphold virtue, and condemn vice. He was in reality the creator of the pure Italian language, and to-day even Italians need almost a special education to be able to understand his exquisite metaphors, grand similes, and marvelous richness and

redundancy of speech. His life was begun in liberty,
it finished in exile, but he has given to the world a
poem that can never die; and the greater the
scholar to-day, the more profound is his reverence and
admiration for Dante. No one will ever again write
a " Divina Commedia."

Longfellow, who understands, in an eminent
degree, translation as an art, yet had a deeper insight
into the hearts of authors. He interpreted by intui-
tion and poetic sentiment, not by the mere medium
of vulgar verse. It is impossible to do the great
Italian poet justice in a foreign tongue, but of all
pretenders the sweetest rhythm has followed Longfellow's lines, and the most comprehensive description of Dante's meaning is embodied in some of our
own poet's words. He worshiped him, and knew
his songs by heart. Dante's three books of " The
Inferno," " Purgatorio," and " Paradiso" have furnished thought and material for writing to hundreds
of poets during six centuries. Dante died in Ra-
venna the fourteenth of September, 1321, thus ending a life which has been of greatest use to the

world. Although in itself unequal, disappointing and misguided, it was not, as he expressed it, a failure.

Before leaving, a delightful half hour was spent with the autograph album. There were letters of George Washington, pages from Carlisle, Emerson, Hawthorne, Chas. Sumner, Dean Stanley, Agassiz, Alfred Tennyson, Charles Dickens, Oliver Wendell Holmes, Bayard Taylor, Rossini, Jenny Lind, Nilsson, and a host of others. They had been cared for by the poet's own hands, and were carefully and neatly pasted in a beautiful book.

Longfellow looked it over with me, and showed almost as much curiosity in it as I did. He looked lovingly at the well-known pages, and stopped here and there to comment on the person, or the character of their calligraphy.

I never before had seen so wonderful a collection of autographs and autograph letters, and promised myself the pleasure of going through it again at no distant day. The professor closed the book with an affectionate smile, and said :

" You must look at it quite carefully the next time.
We will go over it together, and I will explain all in
it that you do not understand. Some of the letters
are very curious, some piquant, and many quite
beautiful. Others, as you see, are merely invitations
and notes. I must confess to the general weakness,
if weakness it be. I love to look at autographs, and
this book is one of my treasures."

CHAPTER IV.

LONGFELLOW'S CHARACTER.

> " Live I, so live I,
>   To my Lord heartily,
>   To my Prince faithfully,
>   To my neighbor honestly,
>   Die I, so die I."
>
>   LAW OF LIFE.

> "Intelligence and courtesy not always are combined ;
>   Often in a wooden house a golden room we find."
>
>   ART AND TACT.

> "I ask myself, is this a dream ?
>   Will it all vanish into air ?
>   Is there a land of such supreme
>   And perfect beauty anywhere ?"
>
>   CADENABBIA, LAKE OF COMO.

MR. LONGFELLOW has been twice married ; his first wife was the beautiful Miss Potter, of Maine. She died in Rotterdam after five years of wedded life and unalloyed happiness. Some years later Mr. Longfellow espoused Miss Fanny Appleton, of Boston, a lady of rare per-

sonal beauty, splendid family, and of a character
eminently suited to the student and poet husband.
Mr. Longfellow has a happy home, and five children,
two sons and three daughters, the fruit of this second
union. They are now grown up and live at home with
their father, or if not all in the house, at least not far
away. Charles Longfellow, the eldest son, is a
famous yachtsman, and in consequence has passed
many years abroad and cruising in foreign waters.
Mr. Ernest, the second son, is a well-known artist of
great talent and fine tuition in his school of painting.
He is married, and lives in Cambridge, directly in
front of the Craigie mansion. The beautiful trio
portrait of three little girls by Buchanan Read, represents the poet's daughters. The picture is too well
known to need description, but the ladies all bear
the same look that they had in youth, and are
women of rare sweetness and refinement of character.
Miss Alice Longfellow, the eldest, and Miss Annie
live at home, while Miss Edith, the second daughter,
is now Mrs. Dana, the wife of Richard Dana, Jr., the
son of the well-known poet.

Longfellow lives at Cambridge the year round, with the exception of the summer months. These are usually passed at Nahant, a charming sea-side resort, just northeast of Boston, and directly facing Lynn. It is almost a neck of land, and is so retired a spot that not all the world knows of its existence.

Honored with an invitation to visit the poet and his brother-in-law, Mr. Appleton, I actually found myself en route, and was not a little disappointed to see unmistakable signs of rain.

Heinrich Heine poetically says: " *Der Himmel hat eine Thräne geweint ;*" evidently he was not speaking of Boston, for in this case, Heaven not only wept one, but many tears The dark clouds grew darker and the rain began to fall, timidly, softly, and exasperatingly, as it alone knows how to do in London and her sister, the Hub. I can always reconcile myself to a hearty down-pour, but I despise a half-and-half shower that will not come boldly out and acknowledge itself rain, hiding in the skirts of mist and deceiving all the world as to its legitimate intention. I always think that there must be something wrong

overhead, yet I suppose in nature's great plan there
must occasionally be a drizzle.

Perhaps it is heresy, but I am not fond of traveling by water ; however, I allowed myself to be per-
suaded to go by boat. After an hour's run we
stopped, and the refreshing sight of a patch of green
made me anxious to get once more on *terra firma.*
The landing is very unpretentious, yet the feet of
many distinguished people have trodden its simple
boards.

A party approaching, disclosed to view no less a
person than the poet himself, accompanied by his
daughters, with Mr. Nathan Appleton. The ladies
were taking advantage of the wet day to go to town,
my arrival being quite unexpected, on account of the
rain. Begging them not to allow me to interfere
with their plans, I had an agreeable escort back to the
house in the persons of the poet and Mr. Nathan.

Nahant, unlike most sea-side places, is a little
bower of verdure. The coast is cultivated right to
the water's edge. Smiling grasses and ferns lean
lovingly over into the basin, unconsciously giving a

touch of art to nature's generosity. Nothing is so disheartening as a sterile, barren beach, with no sight of trees or vegetation, and only hungry waters lapping remorselessly up on the strand. There is scarcely any seaboard to speak of, and the grounds of the various properties extend quite to the water. They are all in a state of natural vegetation, with clambering vines, trailing sea-weed, and rocks lying up against the banks overgrown with moss and prettiness.

Etretat, on the coast of Normandy, is not unlike Nahant in its retirement and natural beauty. We miss in our American resort the enormous *falaises* (cliffs) that clasp the French village in their embrace and stand boldly out to sea, forming a beautiful beach that is adorned by promenaders. Observed from a distance, it is like an old Gobelin tapestry pictured with living forms of brightness and beauty.

Nahant, without the cliffs, is none the less inviting, and although the tableau is different, its quaint grace still reminds me of Etretat.

The house occupied by the professor is large,

roomy, and unpretentious. It is built of wood, in Italian style, with a broad porticoed terrace completely surrounding it. The front part, facing the street, is two stories in height, and on the first floor French windows open out on the terrace, disclosing to view a velvety grass-plot. The back, with an additional wing, faces the sea, and a sharp descent in the hill gives it three stories on this side. The terrace, thus having the appearance of a high balcony overlooking a picturesque declivity, commands a superb view of the sea and surrounding country.

There is a summer garden, replete with the richest vegetation. A profusion of wild roses and sweet-briar fills the air with perfume, while the many-leaved trees are so vine-entangled that their identity is imperiled by a luxuriant mass of living creepers.

Bacon says, "God Almighty first planted a garden," and in the natural beauty of this one, we perceive the touch of the master hand.

The place has a delightful home air, and like many country houses, the exterior is very simple.

Its interior is scarcely more ostentatious. I say

"like" many houses, yet I think there are few in the world that would make the same effect, being equally unpretentious.

The rooms, like those of the Craigie Mansion, are large, airy, sympathetic, and adorned in the most perfect taste. The prevailing tone is light, the chairs are mostly of bamboo or cane, and the floors are covered with carpets and matting. The walls are hung with fine pictures, embracing a variety of engravings, crayon sketches and water colors.

Some curious painted pebbles, framed in a background of velvet, form a unique and handsome ornament. They are the work of Mr. T. G. Appleton, and are faithful pictures of the surrounding scenery, together with other charming bits made from his sketches. They are remarkably well done, and the miniature size of the figures detracts nothing from their perfection.

There is an air of refinement throughout the house that quickly communicates itself to the visitor, and a suspicious sprinkling, here and there, of the best authors, betrays the presence of the *homme de lettres.*

Money will buy much, but the greatest of earth's treasures, virtue and dignity of mind, are not salable articles. A room may be piled high with carved cases that hold only gaudy bindings and trashy volumes; the paintings thereof may be Rafaelles Guidos, Rembrandts or Carlo Dolces; the carpets the finests that the looms of Persia fabricate; the glasses exhaust the wealth of Venice; the mosaics outvie the Florentine roses themselves, and the statuary reflect the handiwork of Michel Angelo's own chisel, yet the home where intellect is the high priest is richer in adornment than a palace filled with all these, and devoid of the refining influence that permeates a house inhabited by persons of intellect, education, and natural breeding.

Longfellow lives in quiet luxury and elegance, while all the comforts of a real home surround him. Still, he is so much in himself, his very presence and manner are so infinitely more attractive than any article that decorates his dwelling, that the outward forms of wealth are but as dross, when compared with the inner beauties of a God-given mind. One must visit the poet many times before realizing that the four walls contain objects of luxury many and rare, and that here are scattered the thousand and one beautiful things that a man of taste instinctively gathers around him.

While the house in Cambridge is replete with *chef-d'œuvres* inestimable in the world of art, yet never, with a single visit, could one carry away other souvenirs ' than that of a beautiful home and a harmonious household. It is the home of a poet, with the poet a dweller therein, himself the most perfect creation among his household gods.

Longfellow shows, in a thousand ways, that he has no wish to appear other than a well-bred gentleman. The complete absence of ostentation in his person and surroundings is not the least of his charms.

Before I had been long an inmate of his household an almost thorough understanding of the man came to me. That which I had remarked, in a casual

4

visit, as seeming modesty and reticence, now impressed me as an absolute characteristic of the man.

I think, in the history of all poets and distinguished men of letters, some eccentricities of mind, character or person have been remarked. It is also a *pose* among persons whose talent, perhaps genius, have lifted them out of the rut of every-day existence, to feign some startling personality, whether from inordinate vanity, or a wish to be thought eccentric, or whether affected merely from the un-worthy love of being peculiar, has never been explained. The fond cherishing of a false idea about self, carried to extremity, constitutes a glaring fault. It is excused in a professed " genius," simply because the world says " we must overlook this or that little idiosyncrasy, he has so much talent."

A celebrated person, whose name I will not mention, used often to be so fatigued with the cares of the day that evening found him in a state not exactly authorized by Beau Brummel. He received his guests, however, and the charm of his exquisite conversation blinded all to his appearance, with the exception of one—an American. His visit was curtailed to the length of a fashionable call, and on his return home he said, "*Poët ou pas poët, j'aime du linge propre.*" ("Poet or not poet, I like clean linen.")

Longfellow has no eccentricities, except the one of being the only poet in the world who avoids every notoriety, and who is content to live within the bosom of his family, a good father, and a plain, every-day citizen, never thrusting his opinions upon one, never vaunting his own talent, scarcely referring, by word or deed, to anything he has ever written, and ignoring, with delightful modesty, the fact that he is more gifted than any one else in the world.

I ought not to pay him the poor compliment, to say that he does not know himself, yet I have often thought that he really does not, and cannot appreciate his own worth and talent.

How a man with his eminently superior knowledge and education can maintain, in the presence of the highest or lowest, such an absolute lack of self-consciousness, passes comprehension; yet it is so. He is the gentlest and most modest of men, yet, at the same time, clothed with a dignity and self-respect which impresses all, and never once borders on the egotistical.

Bacon says "a man's nature is best perceived in privateness, for there is no affectation in passion, for that putteth a man out of his precepts, and in a new case or experiment, for there custom leaveth him ;" also, "that those are happy men whose natures sort with their vocations."

It is not that Longfellow has forced a habit of softness upon himself. He has ever been unassuming and refined, moderate in all things, and perfectly self-poised. Whatever his inner consciousness of self may be, the outer world rests in profound ignorance and admiration.

Æsop's story of the cat who was changed into a maiden shows how far people can trust their natures. She was in every way a decorous damsel, until a mouse ran out from a corner before her, and from thenceforward the charms of young ladyhood were forgotten, for the cat nature was soon resuscitated into an immortal tabby.

Those who make an effort to appear what they are not, and to completely change "what is born in the bone," might have need of Æsop's warning; but in our poet's case it seems to me entirely lost, and I have only made use of the simile in order to place in greater relief the beauty of his real character. He makes no imposition on a wayward nature, but simply lives out the life that has reached perfection by a continual following up of inherent principle. His aim towards the good, rather than the corrupt, is shown in his observance of the beautiful faith which commands us "to love our neighbor as ourself," the inborn honesty and straightforwardness of his soul, and the well-tempered justice that yields every one his right to be thought an "honest man until he is convicted a thief."

In the smallest as well as greatest circumstances of life Longfellow is incapable of subterfuge, misstatement, clap-trap, or make-believe. He enjoys with real humor anything that is funny while it does not

trespass on the bounds of decency or good taste, but
a suspicion of aught else immediately causes him to
close the almost wholly opened portals of countenance. He retires within himself in a half-anxious
way that shows the infinite sensitiveness and suscep-
tibility of his nature. I do not mean that even the
hardiest person would attempt to say anything in his
presence that could not be said in a fashionable
drawing-room; but Longfellow is peculiar in his
tastes, and many things that would raise a smile in
accepted circles, finds no answering smile in his
heart.

A very good idea of his appreciation of the innocently ridiculous, is in the description of the
æsthetic tea at the house of Frau Kranich, in "Hyperion," commencing with the one hundred and sev-
enty-sixth page.

The Moldavian Prince Jerkin makes his way
through the crowds, being anxious to show off his
English. In his haste he begins with a mistake,
saluting Paul Flemming thus :

"Good-bye! Good-bye! Mr. Flemming," said he,

instead of good evening. "I am ravished to see
you in Ems; nice place; — all that there is of
most nice. I drink my water and am good. Do
you not think the Frau Kranich has a very beautiful
leather?"

Who would ever divine that the prince referred
to the gracious lady's skin?

This chapter is replete with evidences of Longfellow's brightness, and quick appreciation of wit in
others. Near the end of the chapter on " Glimpses
in Cloud Land," the professor speaks on time thus:

"For what is time? The shadow on the dial—
the striking of the clock—the running of the sand—
day and night—Summer and Winter—months,
years, centuries—these are but arbitrary and outward signs, the measure of time, not time itself.
Time is the life of the Soul. If not this, then tell
me, what is Time?"

The professor shrieks this aloud in a high voice,
and the baron, half awakened, hearing the word
" time," innocently exclaims:

"I should think it must be near midnight."

CHAPTER V.

A MORNING'S OCCUPATION.

"Toiling, rejoicing, sorrowing,
  Onward through life he goes;
Each morning sees some task begun,
  Each evening sees it close;
Something attempted, something done,
  Has earned a night's repose."
                    THE VILLAGE BLACKSMITH.

"That with a hand more swift and sure,
  The greater labor might be brought
To answer to his inward thought."
                    THE BUILDING OF THE SHIP.

THE professor is an early riser, and at nine the family assembles for breakfast. The dining-room looks out on the back terrace, and from there beyond to the sea. The weather was beautiful, and the sun poured a continuous shower of iridescent rays into the apart-

[80]

ment. They danced lightly hither and thither, at times making a shining halo above the poet's snowy head, anon falling lightly on the golden braids of Edith, Mrs. Dana, or flinging a defiant aureole above the brow of Mr. T. G. Appleton, who is the poet's *vis-à-vis* at table.

One thing particularly noticeable is the quaint ceremony which is never entirely done away with in this family. Each person addresses the other with well-bred deference, and the familiarity that sometimes excuses a " thanks " or "if you please " among one's own, here is conspicuous for its absence.

Of the poet's own family there were present his two daughters, Miss Annie, the younger, and Mrs. Richard Dana (Edith), and her husband, the second of the " trio," Mr. T. G. and Mr. Nathan Appleton, Mr. Longfellow's brothers-in-law, and among the guests the charming and talented artiste, Miss Susan Hale, and Mr. Craig, of New York.

You may imagine that the fine weather put everybody in good spirits, and the table was enlivened by appropriate small-talk, plans for the day, and the

4*

usual inquiries of how the "night was passed."
Longfellow takes some of the tea before mentioned
at early breakfast, a bit of toast, and perhaps an egg,
either poached or *sur-le-plat.* He eats so little that
one can scarcely perceive of what consists his repast.
He is cheerful, good-humored, and devoid of fancies
as regards his own health, yet never for a moment
treats those of others lightly. Conversation rarely
drags, and the slightest possible break is adroitly
covered by the ready grace of the professor.

The eldest at table, he might be the youngest.
It is impossible to imagine, without having passed
some time in the presence of this wonderful man,
how great are his resources, and what youthful vigor
animates his every thought and action.

While he speaks with the experience of ripened
years, he yet invests every subject with the enthusiasm of Paul Flemming, and the graceful flowing
utterance of a poet. The tender fancies, the soft
expressions and ready imagination of the bard color
all his thoughts, and their outward expression is no
less happy. The most commonplace subjects receive

a new interest, when either argued or discussed by the professor, and no question once entered upon is ever dismissed without its full mete of attention.

After breakfast a general sally takes place through the French window, and the broad balcony is soon peopled with animated faces, foremost among them that of the poet. He sits at a round table drawn up near the edge of the terrace, with a light mantle thrown across his shoulders to protect him from the sea-breeze, which is always strong and brisk at Nahant. The pile of letters and periodicals is almost appalling. The lion's share is his, and he speedily commences his morning's work, in the devastation of the mass. Unlike most people, the poet rarely scans the envelope before opening, in order to know the signature of the letter. He deliberately cuts through the upper ledge with a paper knife, and methodically extracts the inclosed missive.

Occasionally an exclamation will break from his lips, such as, "Dear me," "Just look at this," "How am I to get through so long a letter," etc.,

etc. Many send him original poems begging him
to read them and respond quickly as to his opinion
of their talent, while others, less modest, kindly in-
vite him, after reading, to be good enough to correct or alter the MSS. in any way to suit himself.
The poet attempts to read each effort, and only
when too unworthy does he give up in despair, with
a sigh the luckless MSS. is replaced on the table,
and another taken up, shares the same fate. The
letters requesting autographs are many, and always
responded to with the desired signature.

By the way, what a beautiful calligraphy his is.
Slightly back-handed, with neat, distinct lettering,
prominent capitals, and ingenuous small letters, each
one made in just such a way and with just so much
precision. When he begins writing one detects a
slight undulation in the descending stroke, as if the
strong quill were not quite firmly held for an instant,
then on, steadily, until it finishes each letter with firmness and exactitude. There are no marked signs of
the professional flourisher, no heavily shaded letters,
no inequality in their size. Each figure has careful

justice rendered it, and a perfectly legible, honest handwriting is the result. The vowels are also quite prominent, the consonants all duly weighed. How many in this world commit wholesale robbery in the item of dots and crossing of t's, while a shameful disrespect is vouchsafed more than one of the cabalistic twenty-six that form the glory of our English alphabet.

Many people profess to be able to read character from handwriting. I think in Longfellow's case the task would be an easy one. Would that all the world paid the attention that he does to detail. He evinces a special affection for small things, and nothing worth doing is so trivial that all due attention is not paid it. I never saw a blot upon his paper, a word erased by that species of barred-gate-ism that reminds one of the prisoner's window in the trial by Pontius Pilate, or one of those unhealthy daubs that is the conventional obliteration of a word that has lost its usefulness for the quondam writer.

Longfellow is especially pleased with letters from

children, and when well written he even grows
enthusiastic. He reads and re-reads with pleasure,
and many are the flattering comments that I have
heard after the perusal of some juvenile effort. I
think the poet, while appreciating the honors and
attention received from the old, is no less touched
by the admiration of the little ones. Speaking of
attention, I must say that high or low, rich or poor,
receive the same tribute of courtesy from the poet,
in response to an implied or outspoken compliment.
Whatever comes from the heart appeals directly
to his own delicate sense of feeling, and the slightest
attempt on the part of any one to render himself
agreeable is not lost or unnoticed by him ; on the
contrary, the more faintly manifested the praise, the
greater is his satisfaction. All of the letters addressed to him are more or less complimentary.
Those with the bare-faced element predominating
are received and read in silence, while others of
modified expression seem really to please him.

After the correspondence is gone through with
he turns to the daily papers, and from these to the

magazines and monthlies, of which there is an unending stock. I remember on this particular day he was much amused, and as often shocked, by reading an article on epitaphs that was going the rounds of the papers. Some were given aloud for our benefit, and the comments were one and all noticeable. The professor straightened out the paper, adjusted his glasses, and read with a distinct voice. It was curious to listen to the intonations and the half-deprecative utterance when the thing was too irreverent, also to follow the humorous half-laugh that betrayed itself in his voice when a really witty thing was unearthed. The following are among the amusing ones that the professor read aloud :

ON THOMAS WOODCOCK.

" Here lies the body of Thomas Wood*hen*
The most amiable of husbands, and excellent of men."

N. B.—His real name was Wood*cock*, but it wouldn't come in rhyme.—*His widow.*

ON A BREWER.

" Poor John Scott lies buried here;
Tho' once he was both *hale* and *stout*,
Death stretched him on his *bitter bier*,
In another world he *hops* about."

The following is from a German to a stone-cutter, to be put on his wife's tomb:

" My wife Susum is dead; if she had life till next Friday, she'd been dead shust two weeks. As a tree falls so must she stand. All things is impossible mit God."

THO. KEMP ON SHEEP STEALING.

" Here lies the body of Thos. Kemp
Who lived by wool, but died by hemp;
There's nothing would suffice this glutton,
But, with the fleece, to steal the mutton;
Had he but worked and lived uprighter
He'd ne'er been hung for a sheep biter."

The poet's voice ceased, and he laid down the paper, commenting at the same time upon the great waste of space in the newspapers of to-day, besides the baleful habit of making light of death, and topics that should only suggest serious thought. He said that where one of these so-called curious epitaphs might be admissible, a thousand were irreverent, even sacrilegious; where one was touchingly and innocently amusing, another was simply low, and scarcely comical enough to be interesting. "I often read bits," he said, "that wonderment afterwards causes me to ask 'however can such a thing come to be printed.' Although," adding, with his usual justice, " it is no sign, because I do not appreciate it, that a reason did not exist for its having been written ; and many in the world may like and admire what I could not give a second thought to ; still, I do not in general enjoy levity in connection with sacred subjects."

A slight controversy here ensued, and from epitaphs we veered around to poetry. Up to the present time I had taken but little share in the conversation. A momentary lull gave me a chance to speak, and not interrupt.

" Yes," said I, deliberately, when all had finished, "there is no accounting for the rubbish that will in spite of judicious weeding find its way to publicity ; the authors are never known, and perhaps it is as well. I can at present only call to mind one instance, under the head of poetry, which runs as follows : or " —I stopped with an inquiring look around, and half hesitatingly ventured to retract my implied idea of repeating it. In vain—an earnest " Pray go on," " continue," in which the professor's voice was upper-

most in the chorus, positively insisted on hearing the
aforesaid " rubbish ; " clearing my throat, I began—

> " There was a little durl,
>   And she had a little curl
> That hung in the middle of **her forehead,**
>   When she was dood,
>   She was very dood indeed,
> But when she was bad she was **horrid.**"

I looked up triumphantly as the last line rang out.
Depict, imagine, my confusion when the poet raised
his eyes, and with a faint smile, said : " Why ! those
are my words, are they not, Annie," turning to his
youngest daughter, who at that moment was gracefully coming through the low window opening out
on the terrace, at the same time repeating the identi-
cal rhythm that but a moment before I had signalized
as a sample of " rubbish." Miss Annie looked up
laughingly, and said in her cheery voice, " Why, of
course, papa, that comes in your nursery collection.
Don't you remember when Edith was a little girl and
didn't want to have her hair curled, you took her up
in your arms, and shaking your finger at her, commenced, ' There was a little girl,' " etc., etc.

The poet laughed, they all laughed, and I, in spite of my discomfiture, joined in the general merriment. Had I not insisted strenuously that the " lines went the rounds," and would never die out along with other rubbish, the discovery to me of their real authorship would not have been so awkward ; but to declare to a gentleman's face an opinion which at best could have little real value, and that opinion anything but flattering, tried me sorely. The poet is so good-natured that he said nothing; but it was impossible not to laugh. It was one of those coincidences that occur when least expected. Yet rarely does one "get come up with " in such a brutally matter-of-fact way. I still think my mental equilibrium was greatly disturbed, and my self-esteem dropped lower and lower into the depths of humiliation. Why on earth had I not stumbled on some other simile? But no, to add to my perplexity, Mr. Nathan asked me pleasantly if I " could remember any more of the same kind," and then we all got to laughing in real earnest. It was too funny, and I forgot my own discomfiture in watching the evident enjoyment of the professor.

First, he was grave, then a ripple stole from his lips in a half unconscious way, until finally, yielding to the general impulse toward risibility, it broke irresistibly out like a mountain rivulet. Timidly at first it leaves nature's bed, and as it flows onward, flows itself out ever in greater strength, until it joins a rushing torrent that carries everything before it. Just so is the professor's laugh. Faint at first, then breaking into a series of hearty cadences that give one a pleasant sensation on hearing them; when he finishes, a half sigh follows the last little gurgle, and a homely " dear me, how I do laugh," restores the speaking countenance to its own former likeness.

How few have a sympathetic smile! how few a sympathetic laugh! and again, how many make a sounding-board of the roof of their mouth, which echoes successive shrieks of merriment, while the face expresses any other sentiment than that of fun. Others, vice versa, betray in every feature the half suppressed laughter that threatens momentarily to burst all bounds, and through the natural outlet communicates itself to all present. The world is full of sad hearts and faces, but we welcome with joy the advent of any individual with the natural attribute of a wholesome, hearty, joyous and unconstrained laugh.

Such is the natural gift of God that few are the enviable possessors of, and it is one of the many that endow our great poet. While he rarely expresses his feelings impulsively, he still yields himself up wholly to the charm of the moment, and whatever mirthful deserves a genuine laugh, the professor tenders his tribute with unstint of graciousness, and in so honest a way that it does one's heart good to see and hear him.

How I have wandered from our morning's real business! Apropos of the poem aforesaid, some one suggested to me the thought of revenge, and with a little of the inherent viciousness in woman the suggestion was eagerly carried out, the poet waiting courteously to give me my "*revanche.*" I dared to respond "that my gross blunder was inexcusable, and a possibility of such ever arising in future, could only be avoided in one way. In order not to be mistaken authors must feel the value of putting their name to everything they write, even when that name be ———— Longfellow."

I, with the common herd, cannot always appreciate, but out of deference to a name all the world reveres I would be silent.   Under the circumstances, knowing how and why it came to be written, my " rubbish" transmogrifies itself into a cunning and appropriate ballad.

CHAPTER VI.

LONGFELLOW'S IDEA OF POETICAL INFLUENCE.

" O ye dead Poets who are living still
    Immortal in your verse, though life be fled,
    And ye, O living Poets, who are dead
    Though ye are living, if neglect can kill,
    Tell me if in the darkest hours of ill,
    With drops of anguish falling fast and red
    From the sharp crown of thorns upon your head,
    Ye were not glad your errand to fulfill ?
    Yes: for the gift and ministry of song
    Have something in them so divinely sweet,
    It can assuage the bitterness of wrong;
    Not in the clamor of the crowded street,
    Not in the shouts and plaudits of the throng,
    But in ourselves, are triumph and defeat."

THE POETS.

THIS morning we took a little walk, and the poet, who had slept well, seemed, strange to say, nervous, and ill at ease.

This feeling soon wore off, for who, in the presence of so delightful a family party, could

long "sit in sadness"? After breakfast, he was enlivened by numerous visitors, and sat on the balcony
receiving his guests with great vivacity and evident
pleasure. From the adjoining library I could hear
his voice, now in earnest, now in lighter talk, but
more than usually gay.

It seemed scarcely a wholesome humor, however,
and I could frequently detect a nervous rising in
the vibrating tones, that was not habituary. Having no part in the conversation I could not listen, or
even stay in my corner when my work was finished,
so I stole away until we met at luncheon.

He seemed in a peculiarly restless state, and
spoke with quick precision, and in an outspoken
manner that was even beyond his usual terseness,
so I wondered of what he could have been thinking. He ate, as usual, the slightest possible amount
of food, and seemed watchful of every word that
was uttered at table. We adjourned to the drawing-
room accompanied by Mr. Nathan Appleton, and
Mr. Craig, a young gentleman who was visiting the
poet at the time, and in a few moments the general

conversation began. There were some fresh flowers on the table, and thinking one to be a camellia, I remarked upon its odorless beauty, and asked the poet if he had ever read " La Dame aux Camélias," by Alexander Dumas, Jr. He spoke up quickly, answering,

" No; I commenced it, but could not continue, as it seemed to me a book for unhealthy appetites. I doubt not there is much that is fine in it, as Dumas is a man of extraordinary imagination and skill, but I cannot bring myself to read such works as 'La Dame aux Camélias.' "

He went on with increasing warmth,

" Now, there is another French writer whose books have probably been read by millions, but to whose writing I can never turn with pleasure. I speak of Alfred de Musset, a man with a God-given, beautiful talent, but all for the bad. I often think of what he might have done in the world, had his mind been on anything pure or virtuous. Look at ' Rolla ' ' une nuit de Mai,' could more inspired or exquisite language have found its way into

5

verse? yet mark the intent of the poem. I read,
and read on, half fascinated by the flowing grace,
passion and eloquence of his rhythm, then some
startling outburst of infidelity shocks me so that
I leave the book with horror, and say to my
soul, 'How sad! a beautiful talent gone to waste; a
brilliant imagination seeing only the spectacle of
ribaldry and infamy; a bright spark of genius,
growing and passing its life grovelling amongst the
tares of a dissolute and morally unhealthy clime.'
He is to me a heart-rending example of the uses to
which a man may dedicate a great gift originally of
divine import, whose whole life and writings are
made up of worldliness, license and innate cravings
after unhealthy mental food. His words pander
to the vilest taste, while the beauty with which he
clothes his ideas is undeniable. Even in some of
his most violent outbursts, he does not divest his
pages of charm, and exquisite wording. He seems
to have lived with a gloss of utter indifference to
any faith covering a soul that I have often hoped
was not so barren as he himself painted it. I de-

plore with my whole heart such a mistaken life, that had within it the wherewith to be something great and true. Only think! had he described good with the eloquence and sincerity that he bestowed on vice, what a benefit he would have been to the world, and what a series of powerful arguments he would have wielded for mankind, with a brain and pen that followed each other in such a headlong torrent of irresistible poetry? One might overlook an occasional skepticism, but no one with any respect for virtue and goodness could remain unmoved while reading any one of his poems. His fanatical tendency to scoff and laugh to scorn the slightest thing that is good, is a terrible power in the hands of a man of genius. As a student I read, but as a God-fearing man, I lament."

Never had I heard the poet speak with greater warmth, and so anxious was I to hear more, that when he continued the subject of poets and poetical license, I took the liberty of defending them in a moderate way.

"You are wrong," he said, decidedly, " when

one finds in writing that his imagination is running away with him, it is time to stop ; I always did."

"Yes," said I, quickly, "you show in your writings often—" but I stopped shamefacedly. Did I dare to criticise Longfellow ?

He looked up eagerly and said,

"Pray, don't stop; what were you going to remark about my writings ? I should like your opinion." Then he assumed a curious attitude of interest and impatience.

I could not back out ingloriously, so went on :

"In your writings I find a want of *laisser aller*, that in the poetic sense often hastens a climax. When, by some outburst of passion, you work your reader up to fever heat, you quietly leave the dangerous ground, and instead of an unlimited outpour of intense feeling, one has to be satisfied with simpler and more modified expressions. Still even you, yourself, cannot always hide the deep under-current of passion that runs surreptitiously through your verse, and almost threatens, at times, to break the bounds."

"But it never does," interrupted the poet, excitedly. "I understand what you mean, but I always try, whenever my fancy leads me on, to have a due regard for outward form. I could not write that which poetic license permits if it goes against my conscience and teachings. But pray let us speak of some one else rather than myself, although you will understand, some day, why I speak thus."

Mr. Nathan Appleton came up and touched my shoulder, for with the poet's words we had risen, and as I supposed, conversation for that day was at an end. I was just going out when his brother-in-law spoke.

"You have told him the truth," he said, "and I think, in twenty years, no one has ever said as much to him; but mind, he has not finished with you, and to-morrow, or later to-day, you will have his answer."

He then went out, and I returned to my room to reflect on what I had said almost too abruptly to the dear old poet. I had often thought of this, yet never dreamed that, in the heat of conversation, my headlong talk would have resulted in such plain speaking.   I realized how much superior to all things was this man's sense of right and honor, and how, perhaps, he had, at times, sacrificed many an idea that would have formed, in Byron, an innocent glory.   Before going in to dinner, we met on the terrace.   He came directly to me, put out his hands, and said, with a sweet voice but reproachful accents,

" You speak with the enthusiasm of youth, but even had I the inclination, one could scarcely expect me to lie awake at night writing things that would set a bad example to a class of thirty young men whom I had to teach in the morning.   Heaven be praised ! I tried at least to be guided by the right spirit."

I was not surprised with the poet's outspoken words regarding Alfred de Musset, for any one who had ever known Longfellow and the June atmosphere of his home-life, could readily understand his condemnation of that poet's mode of living, and the unsavory sentiment with which his poems were filled.

De Musset lived at a time when virtue was almost a fiction in France, and his dissolute habits, and constant companionship with scoffers and unbelievers, was not calculated to turn his mind readily into a better channel. He was born the eleventh of December, 1810, in the old part of Paris, in a street near the Hotel Cluny. The house still bears the number, 33 Rue des Noyers. He died a little past midnight of May .1, 1857, two months after his reception and entrance into the French Academy. At the age of forty-seven, brilliant in all intellectual attainments, but physically a wreck, the life that had been so full of promise and bright hopes, and so covered with questionable glory, was sapped at its roots by the grim monster, consumption, and at an early day his family feared he would be one of its victims. His poetic taste showed itself at a very tender age, and before he was eighteen he had already published something of account. "Rolla" is one of his most touching poems, others also breathe, in certain lines, a spirit of unbelief and atheism appalling to read, and sad to think about as coming from the soul of a young man divinely gifted. He was only twenty-three when this was published in the famous Parisian monthly, " *Revue des deux Mondes*," and from that time forth his works followed each other in quick succession. "Fortunio," "la Nuit de Mai," "la Nuit de Décembre," " To Ninon," " A Confession," " A Letter to Lamartine," several plays, " Caprice," a translation of Shakespeare's " As you Like It " (comme il vous plaira), a quantity of lesser, but more " spirituelle " efforts, and in a second volume of poems, I can readily understand his own preference, given to his strongest works—"le Fils de Titien," " Lorenzaccio," and " Carmosine." Besides these, with prolific and unimpaired talent, he wrote, until his death, numerous sonnets, essays and letters, all with exquisite poetic rhythm, but most of them tainted with the dreadful impurity of thought and association that distinguishes Alfred de Musset from a great galaxy of French writers, the most talented, the most brilliant, but the most hardened. He, among few, may fully claim the title " genius," as no late writer of the nineteenth century has ever compared with, or exceeded the beauty of his language, or style of writing. Victor Hugo is unapproachable, the acknowledged king of French poets, and in speaking of others one should always remember that he takes precedent. They can only come after, but Alfred de Musset follows closely in his footsteps. He gave to the world so striking an example of poetic talent, that he may be considered as the second light in the French firmament of literature. Perhaps, as Longfellow said, had his own every-day life been different, one might have discovered a healthier tone in his mind pictures. His mode of living must have been singularly abasing to the intellect, and harassing to the mental and physical resources of the man. His nights were spent in feasting and orgy; his days in preparing for the following night. His truest friends were his own family, but he paid little attention to them. He probably never knew the refining influence of the love of one good woman, and even his " maîtresses " were fickle, unfaithful, and interested. No wonder that one of his fitful genius and unsatia-

5*

ble appetite for sensational scenes, to-day enjoyed
the society of ladies such as Pauline Viardot, and
to-morrow wept tears of sorrow at an inflexible
Ninon. His whole existence, from the time when
he left college until his death, seemed one raging
whirlpool of immoderate excess, with the sentiments
in his soul warring and clashing with one another.
He seemed penetrated by ugliness as by beauty, and
as fascinated with one as with the other ; he extolled
virtue with the same breath that he encouraged vice,
and to everything, good or bad, he lent the charm of
his inimitable verse, and wrote, alas, with equal
enthusiasm and brilliancy, no matter what the moral
tendency of his subject, and no matter in what questionable light it presented the author to the world.
Few writers would dare say what Longfellow has
said, yet with tender pity for a misled life, and due
appreciation of the marvelous influence that one
with "a divine talent" might have exercised, had he
chosen to employ his gifts for the benefit of mankind. Longfellow may be a Puritan in one sense of
the word, but while the life of the one is a long

hymn of praise to the great Maker, that of the other is lost in the maelstrom of discord and unevenness. It spent itself in a short blaze of transcendent glory, and was soon obliterated within a pall of densest smoke. So lives the name and memory of Alfred de Musset. His genius will beguile, but his works will ever grate on those who find life, as does Longfellow, beautiful in Faith, Hope and Charity.

CHAPTER VII.

LONGFELLOW'S APPRECIATION OF PARODY.

"True, his songs were not divine;
　　Were not songs of that high art,
　Which, as winds do in the pine,
　　Find an answer in each heart;
　　　　But the mirth
　　　　Of this green earth
　Laughed and reveled in his line."

OLIVER BASSELIN.

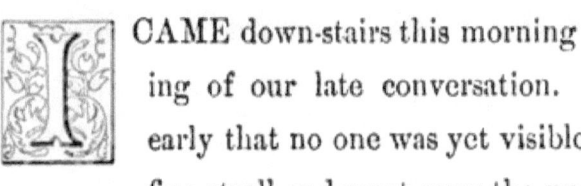 CAME down-stairs this morning still think-
ing of our late conversation. It was so
early that no one was yet visible, so I had a
fine stroll and went over the pretty garden
so overrun with its wealth of verdure. All the while
my mind kept running on the poet, and the various
conversations that we had had. I went to the foot of
the garden and cautiously descending a very narrow
path, prepared to lean over and dip my hands in the
salt water that came purring up so lovingly against

the domesticated rocks. They stood there, grim old things, as if all their life consisted in growing old gracefully, with a quantity of green vines hanging to them, enlivened by the daily conversation of the sea, and the friendly waves that dashed up to say "good morning ;" with a few old family friends like moss and sea-weed, who never left them, and who added, to the obligation of finding a shelter, the eternal one of staying there forever.

While I was slipping and turning about, I was startled by a hearty *"Bon jour!"* and a pleasant laugh.

Looking up, I saw the professor at his open window, looking very youthful, and gazing down upon me. My decidedly ungraceful attitude must have excited his risibilities, for he looked highly amused at something and said quickly, as I glanced about me,

"Oh, don't go away, I am coming down directly."

I made a great effort and clambered back to meet him on a more substantial footing.

The sight of nearly all the family gathered on the balcony, reminded me that perhaps I had been a little long in my solitary rambling, and breakfast was ready, so I retraced my footsteps towards the house. I met the professor in the front hall, and we went into the parlor where the table was laid out, and, as I had half divined, waiting.

The poet was very agreeable, and congratulated me on my early rising.

"I am up betimes, myself," he said, "but I am afraid that you have outdone me this morning, however. No matter how late I am up at night, I never can sleep later the following morning. I usually wake up about the same hour, eight o'clock."

While we sat at table Mr. Appleton began one of his cheerful anecdotes. I laughed, and he said,

"Pray now, madam, don't say that you have heard it before, as you would spoil a good story for the rest of us."

Touched by such a picture I decided to sacrifice myself, and he continued his recital.

"Your asking if I had heard it," I said, " reminds

me of something very funny, but 1 do not know that I can tell it without offending the poet. It is a parody on one of his poems."

"One of my poems?" said Longfellow; "I would be delighted to hear it rather than offended. 1 beg you will repeat it."

So I began :

"A long time ago I went to see a comical musical farce in the theater, where some people traveling on the Rhine pass a dull evening with snatches of song, quotations from famous authors, &c. One of the travelers asked to entertain the company, gets up and begins—

"'Lives of great men all remind us,'

"The other quietly interrupts, 'I know the lines.' But the speaker, continues,

"'We can make our lives sublime,"

"Vigorous interruption from the same source, '*I know the lines !*'

"The unabashed reciter keeps composedly on—

" ' And in dying leave behind us '

" Threats and outcries from the man who interrupts,

" ' I KNOW THE LINES ! '

" Then together they joined hands, went into the
steps of a break-down, and shrieked at the full pitch
of their lungs,—

> " ' And in dying leave behind us
>   Foot-prints with our seven-by-nines.' "

That was enough for the poet. He broke into
shouts of laughter, and said :

" Dear me, how very funny ! And to think that
I, who wrote the original, never conceived so *soul-
stirring* an end for that verse."

" It is not to be wondered at," said some one
present, " your feet are too small to have suggested
it."

" Although," interrupted the poet, " my feet generally fill the meter." (Meter is the French for
yard.)

After that, the expression "I know the lines," became a household word.

The poet continued laughing until the tears came into his eyes, and he blamed himself for being, as he said, so childish. Seeing that he enjoyed parody, I told him about an evening at the house of a countess, in Verona, when poor Dante had a new rendering given by the young Count P——.

Without changing a word, he commenced,

"Nel mezzo del cammin di nostra vita mi ritrovai per una selva oscura," etc., etc., "che la diritta via era smarrita," and gave the words such a peculiar reading, accompanied by appropriate gestures, that everybody shouted with laughter; at the word "vita" (waist, in English), he spanned his own soldier-like dimensions with such effeminate glee that the double meaning of the word was fully apparent. But the climax was reached when he prepared to commence the third stanza.

Clearing his throat he began to talk, but stopped as if encountering something that tasted peculiar. He kept on working his face into such terrible grimaces, anon rolling his eyes, scraping his tongue, and finally dropping a frantic hand over the pit of his stomach with a gesture of such utter despair, that nobody was surprised when the words came out. With a last awful shudder, and in a hysterical shrill voice, he screamed, " Tanto è amaro, che poco era piu morte ——"

Before I could finish the professor was convulsed; he said, " No wonder."

" 'Tanto è amaro,' is bitter enough in Dante's own forcible language, yet see how without changing a word the line has a different meaning when accompanied by such vivid gestures. I laugh now, what would it have been had I been in Verona that evening?"

Longfellow, who had followed the thread of the story, was prepared for it, but he had the fit on, and could not control his emotion. As soon as he recovered his breath he would break out anew, and finally, when his strength was exhausted, he said,

" It is really terrible to parodize a man like

Dante, yet it is funny, and I must enjoy it in spite of the source."

"Now," said Mr. Nathan, "that we are on the subject of parodies, you must hear Mr. Longfellow on his own poems. I think they are too funny not to be honored with a mention. Once my nephew Charles came to pay us a visit, when we resided in Lynn; I think about fifteen years ago. He would come in a sail-boat, but as the water was fearfully high, the frail bark capsized, and Master Charles got a good ducking. When he reached our house he was a sorry, wet-looking fellow enough, and, of course, had to change his clothes. I loaned him a pair of slippers which he wore home in lieu of boots, and the next day a neat parcel came over from Nahant, with the following lines written on the outside in Mr. Longfellow's hand:

> "'Slippers that perhaps another,
>   Sailing o'er the bay of Lynn,
> A forlorn or shipwrecked nephew
>   Seeing, may purloin again.'"

A roar of laughter greeted Mr. Appleton's recitation, and we all agreed that the poet himself "knew the lines."

"That is not all," added Mr. Nathan ; "I remember some other verses, not parody exactly, but extremely funny, and I am sure you would all like to hear them. Permit me," turning to the poet.

"Nay," said Mr. Longfellow, half shamefacedly, "I think that I am becoming too prominent, and perhaps ——"

"There are no perhaps's," returned Mr. Nathan, "I must tell this. When my father was traveling in Switzerland, a long time ago, having postilions, footmen, etc., the bills were frightful, and in Zurich, even heavier. My father had already written his name in the visitors' books with compliments for the lovely place, and when his bill was brought in he regretted his undue haste and amiability. Mr. Longfellow came up and said,

"'Pray, let me add my autograph and treat the landlord as he merits.'

"The inn was called 'The Raven,' and Mr. Longfellow wrote the following in his book :

> " ' Beware of the Raven of Zurich,
>   'Tis a bird of omen ill,
>   With an ugly, unclean nest
>   And a very, *very* long bill.' "

This time even the professor had to laugh. He remembered the circumstance too well to forget the impression made on his mind by the landlord's extortion, and he added to Mr. Nathan's words these: "I am afraid that .page wherein those lines are inscribed is not the first shown to the visitors at 'The Raven.' I never went there again, but surely we shall never forget Zurich."

Our parodies ended with a quotation from an English paper, on " Hiawatha :"

> "Should you ask me, What's its nature ?
>   Ask me, What's the kind of poem ?
>   Ask me in respectful language,
>   Touching your respectful beaver,
>   Kicking back your manly hind-leg,
>   Like to one who sees his betters;
>   I should answer, I should tell you,
>   'Tis a poem in this metre,
>   And embalming the traditions,
>   Fables, rites, and superstitions,
>   Legends, charms, and ceremonials
>   Of the various tribes of Indians,

From the land of the Ojibways,
From the land of the Dacotahs,
From the mountains, moors, and fenlands
Where the heron, the Shuh-shuh-gar,
Finds its sugar in the rushes:
From the fast-decaying nations,
Which our gentle Uncle Samuel
Is improving very smartly,
From the face of all creation,
Off the face of all creation.

" Should you ask m , By what story,
By what action, plot, or fiction,
All these matters are connected?
I should answer, I should tell you,
Go to Bogue and buy the poem,
Published, neatly, at one shilling,
Published, sweetly, at five shillings."

CHAPTER VIII.

LONGFELLOW VISITS JULES JANIN.

"A millstone and the human heart are driven ever round,
    If they have nothing else to grind, they must themselves
        be ground."
                                    THE RESTLESS HEART.

"Perchance the living still may look
    Into the pages of this book,
    And see the days of long ago,
    Floating and fleeting to and fro."
                        END TALES OF A WAYSIDE INN.

THE rain commenced to fall about noon, and we were in for a wet day. No one could go out of doors, and even the favorite terrace was so deluged with salt spray and mist, that it was quite unsafe.

The professor was very well, and seemed to enjoy the gloomy down-pour.

[119]

I was visibly reminded of his exquisite poem, and said softly to myself :

" The day is cold, and dark and dreary."

He interrupted me :

" You are trying to flatter me," said he, smiling ; " still you must know that that is one of my favorite poems."

I continued to repeat a portion, until he looked up with a quick sense of humor, and said :

" I know the lines !"   After that we all laughed, and there were no more poetic quotations.

After luncheon we again assembled in the drawing-room, and commenced a talk and discussion on things in general.

Longfellow is a charming conversationalist, and it was peculiar that while he spoke, with the greatest beauty and ease, seven languages, he never interlarded a word from one tongue into a conversation held in another.   If English, it was all English, with beautiful round phrases, and the choicest of words. If necessary to use one of the many expressions that have become familiar to the Anglo-Saxon, he even then translated it immediately, which gave an adequate idea of his exactitude in speech, and the value he set upon his mother tongue.

He spoke of his visit to Paris as a student, and a call on Jules Janin.

"I went up five flights of terrible stairs," he said, "and when you have seen some of those houses in the Quartier Latin (Latin quarter), you may imagine what those particular stairs were like. I rapped on a door, as there was no bell-rope visible, and a smiling maid showed me into a very small antechamber, and from thence into a modest parlor, study and dining-room, all in one.

"The greatest confusion reigned everywhere, and the master of the house, sitting among his household gods, was the greatest study of all.

"He greeted me with French effusion, and a pen in his hand, freshly dipped in ink—turned around with such vivacity that a large drop splashed almost in my face. He half dragged me into a chair which he said looked uninviting, but was really very com-

G

fortable. He then called some one, with a clear voice. A very young lady came into the apartment. She was introduced as Madame Janin, and I had barely time to look at her when he started up and said, ' Now that you are come, we will have dinner.'

" I did not see where we would have it, but he smiled with delight, saying, ' Watch me,' and I did.

" He swept everything off the table on the floor in the corner of the room, and with great glee announced the banqueting board ready.

" The maid came in, quickly laid the cloth, and before I realized it a steaming soup was on the table. He insisted on putting me in front of him, and madame at his right.

" The soup was a very excellent pot-au-feu, and' although a little bewildered by the rapid way in which things had come about, I was a hungry student, and did not need a second invitation.

" Jules Janin was a very bright man, with a good disposition, and exceedingly gay. He talked about Paris life and women in a way that amazed me, and all with an air of perfect propriety that was astound-

ing. The more surprised I was to see the meek
young woman who sat at his side, laugh with him
and enjoy jokes that I could not listen to without
blushing. He rattled them off with such infinite
zest that I began to think something had been amiss
with my education, as I seemed not to appreciate
them in the right way. He was debonair and friendly
with the madame, often stopping in the midst of his
speech to pat her cheek, call her his dear little cab-
bage, or smile upon her with an affection that was
quite charming to see. She never spoke, and seemed,
however, beyond this quite a nonentity.

"Well, this dinner was one of startling surprises to
me. I thought then that I enjoyed it, and I did—the
eating part, but the looseness of the conversation
scarcely compared favorably with what I had been
accustomed to. Towards the dessert, he became
more serious, and I listened to his really brilliant
remarks with great pleasure.

"He gave me much very useful information, and I
have since seen how true were his sayings in one
sense. When we had finished our coffee, he sug-

gested a stroll, and we went out into the streets. I
said 'good-bye' to madame, and wondered if she
were going to be left alone in the house, but Mr.
Jules, without the slightest compunction, tapped her
on the shoulder in sign of adieu, and we started.

"It was a beautiful night, and we walked a long
way by the Seine, and near the great Notre Dame
cathedral, whose towers were bathed in moonlight.
The night was so charming that we continued our
promenade for more than three hours, up and
down.

"Janin's character, while brilliant, was unsafe, or
so it appeared to me—for he was shockingly legér or
trivial, and his talk, while one moment witty and
delightful, the next was reeking with some French
story that completely horrified me. When I bade
him good-bye I thought I would not willingly see
him again. In fact, many years passed, when I met
him once on the Boulevard of Paris.

"He was but little changed, and again wanted me
to dine with him. I was pleased to meet him, and
my own experience in the meantime had taught me

that Frenchmen are not as bad at heart as they make themselves out to be.

"Accepting his invitation, I found him in another apartment, more ample and splendid, perhaps, but still disorder was the reigning queen as before.

"He introduced me to Madame Janin.

"I, expecting to renew my acquaintance of former times, found to my astonishment that she had changed beyond recognition, and I tried in vain to recall her to my memory. I got through the form of saying good evening, however, and later on expressed my surprise to find madame so different from what I remembered her.

"'When did you meet her,' said he, eagerly.

"'Why, let me see,' I pondered, 'I should think about nine or ten years ago, and since then she is wonderfully altered.'

"'Great Heavens,' said he, seriously, 'are you jesting? did you think this the same one? Who knows how many Madame Janin's there have been during that time?'

"I looked up quietly.

"'And this one,' said I, coldly.

"'Ah, ha!' he shrieked, with a shrewd laugh. 'This time, mon cher, I have been caught my-self, and the real Madame Jules Janin stands before you;' but, with a sober look, 'apropos of our little dinner in the Quartier Latin, nothing to my wife of that, I beg, otherwise your evening to-night might be less tranquil.'

"I never saw him again," said Longfellow, "and I think that is one of the first and last French literary 'ménages' that I frequented. Janin thought it a fine joke, but I see no beauty or decency in such an irregular life, although he had many a laugh at what he called 'my puritanical innocence.'"

It was easy to see that remembrances of this sort made a great impression on Mr. Longfellow, and while he always rendered full justice to the talent and attainments of the person, the character and daily habits of the man were to him a special study. He could not, with his severe puritanical ideas, accept or form any intimacy with one whose life was made up of condensed experience in vice, and the careless way of living day after day in the same unhealthy moral atmosphere that usually falls to the lot of men of letters, especially in Paris.

Jules Janin died some years ago, and later the "real" madame followed him. He was really "caught," as he said, although his wife was so clever that she revenged all of her predecessors, and was fond enough of Jules to write (so the wicked world says) many of his most renowned criticisms. He never left *her* alone in the evening with a careless pat on the cheek, but almost begged permission to go out, and in spite of his former license he really became "regular."

I told this to the poet.

"Yes," he quickly said, "all is right, with one exception.

"I don't believe that madame ever wrote a line of his works, as he was quite clever enough to do all, and more, than he ever did, himself."

That speech was so like Longfellow. Although

he could not admire his character, and the man was dead, he would still do him justice in his heart, and spoke out in his defense with his rare honesty and beautiful love of truth.

Being on the subject of writers he got back to poets, and he spoke of Swinburne.

"I must admire such an avalanche of passionate verse," said he, "but I am no way affected by his fiery writings.

"The man is undoubtedly a remarkable character in his way, but, must I confess it? it is a way that I do not like. His words seem to me to breathe forth a pestilential fire, as impetuous as Vesuvius and as fatal, and on reading one has still ringing in their ears the clash of natures that rage against each other, and the inharmonious din that accompanies such energetic poetry.

"Some of the descriptions are fine, and very vivid, but the whole leaves my soul in turmoil and wearies me beyond expression.

"How different is Byron, who, while the incarnation of voluptuous verse, still offends in a sweeter manner and often soothes while he disturbs. I cannot commend him entire," said he, quickly, " neither has he the right to wholesale condemnation ; but, where one can choose many passages of equal beauty and intense emotional quality, it is easy to leave the rest alone, although the grade of passion is equal, in expressing them both, while the thought and reading are infinitely less pure, and different one from the other.

" In all other poets of volcanic attributes this one great quality is ambiguous ; in Byron it is almost a charm, and then too he was —— Byron.

" Of Dante and Shakespeare," he continued, " I will not speak. You know all men have their idols, they are mine."

CHAPTER IX.

LONGFELLOW WITH HIS GRANDCHILD.

> " I have you fast in my fortress
> And will not let you depart,
> But put you down in the dungeon
> In the round tower of my heart.
> And there will I keep you forever;
> Yes, forever, and a day,
> Till the walls shall crumble to ruin
> And moulder in dust away."
>
> THE CHILDREN'S HOUR.

> " O child! O new-born denizen
> Of life's great city, on thy head
> The glory of the morn is shed
> Like a celestial benison !
> Here at the portal thou dost stand,
> And with thy little hand
> Thou openest the mysterious gate
> Into the Future's undiscovered land."
>
> TO A CHILD.

> " ' Strike the sails !' King Olaf said;
> 'Never shall men of mine take flight;

[130]

Never away from battle I fled!
Never away from my foes,
Let God dispose
Of my life in the fight.'"
KING OLAF'S WAR HORSE. —TALES WAYSIDE INN.

HE family party was complete, and after breakfast the balcony was full of bright faces. Everybody appeared in the best of health and spirits, and even baby in his carriage crowed with joy and juvenile ecstasy.

Mrs. Dana, "Edith," is his mother. She retains the same beautiful features that lent such a charm to her babyhood, and the "little curl that hung in the middle of her forehead," has retired with womanly dignity to join her sister locks on either side of her winsome face. She has violet-blue eyes, a skin of cream and roses, a dainty, shapely nose, a most lovable mouth, and fine masses of ashen blonde hair, that undulate away from the temples and are crowned by a glistening braid.

She is extremely vivacious and fond of argument. Mr. T. G. Appleton has left his pebbles to join us, and his advent is always welcome.

I never knew a man more thoroughly original than Mr. Appleton, and whatever he says is just characteristic of himself. His fund of anecdotes is inexhaustible, and each day his clever sayings and ingenious reflections are tempered with wholesome humor. Mrs. Dana always answers "Uncle Tom" back, as Mr. Appleton is called, and many bright flashes of *esprit* are the result.

The poet looks on amusedly, lovingly, and with an enjoyment that is undeniable. He rarely interrupts, but when referred to as umpire gives a gracious decision, that instead of settling the matter in full throws an entirely new light on the subject, and also throws both parties off the track.

This wary and dexterous way of answering a question is one of the professor's great points, or "coups," as the French would say. From being an innocent umpire, he becomes, with one of his adroit remarks, a master in the art of drawing others out.

The professor's face is a study, while those impromptu word skirmishes are going on.

Whether the subject be grave or gay, he listens

with the same seriousness, and his face glows with vigilance and watchful interest. He seems like a general at the head of his forces, and only by the color that faintly comes and goes in his cheeks, and the quick changing light of his flashing eye, can one discover that he is at all moved.

He reminded me forcibly of the late King Victor Emanuel of Italy.

At a review of many thousand troops given outside the famous arena of Milan, a few weeks previous to the first and welcome visit of the German emperor to Italy, in 1875, I had an opportunity of watching, during an hour, the great soldier king, the head of the house of Savoy. How magnificently he sat his horse, and with what royal grace and favor did he look upon an army that is the honor and pride of Italy. It was during the mock cavalry charge that the king was to me perfectly fascinating. The men rushed forward with such force and vigor that numbers of poor fellows were unhorsed, and the cry of "*nomo a terra*" (men to earth) rang with too

great frequency upon the air to realize that it was
only a make-believe battle.

His Majesty the King never moved a muscle,
but his glance ran like lightning along the lines,
and the bronzed face, although set with a terrible
composure, yet glowed with color and interest. Not
a sound escaped his lips, nor did the long ends of
his waxed mustache betray the slightest nervous
motion. With calm, superb mien he sat and gazed
upon a sight that would have moved most men,
his face only betrayed the kingly pride and adaman-
tine composure that he possessed in so eminent a
degree.

His flashing eye pierced to the farthest extent of
the Piazza d'Armi, always accompanied with the
same marvelous quietness of feature. The white-
gloved hand never wavered as it loosely held the
rich bridle-rein, and during the whole of the charge,
he never moved from his graceful position.

The royal saddle-cloth, with its broidered corners
and fringed edges, was held down with such firmness
that one would have thought it a part of the trap-

pings and paraphernalia of a warrior cast in bronze rather than a breathing embodiment of a real, live king. One forgot his person in looking at his royal head, military *tenue*, and martial bearing.

He was every inch a soldier, and the great general at the head of his troops. ·They say that no one ever sat a horse as did Victor Emanuel, and certainly I shall never forget how I saw him that day, the fierce Italian sun pouring down on his gilded helmet, the large Piazza d'Armi covered with the brilliant and magnificently-trained army, and the clouds of dust thickening the air almost as with the smoke of great cannonading.

Who can wonder that the son of Carlo Alberto was adored by his people; that while " Il Re Galantuomo" was all that was kingly and royal, he was loved so much the more as a man, because the brave soldier came first in the hearts of his subjects?

Those who see United Italy to-day realize the great work accomplished by a man who, while never forgetting that the blue blood of a long-lined ancestry coursed through his veins, fought with the ardor of a common soldier. He endured toil and hardships, and in the thickest of the fight mingled freely the royal vesture with the modest uniform of the peasant. Together the sabers clashed that ransomed a people from the oppressor's power, and purchased a unity that shows to-day how greater than any other European nation is the progress of modern Italy. Besides being a most honest man, the king was one of such wondrous personal fascination that every one of his people who came in contact with him left his presence a firmer adherent, a passionate adorer, and a most loyal subject forevermore. Such was the man who governed with honesty and simplicity, with heart and brain, and who merited the title of "The Honest King" (Il Re Galantuomo).

I have often thought of him, and the expression on his face that day. Physically there was not the slightest resemblance between the two, yet Longfellow had the same look of conscious power, with complete control of his features, and the skilled and modest composure that so beautifully becomes the truly great.

I think the poet is generally happiest in the morning. It is a sort of pleasurable omen when the night has passed well, and to the affectionate inquiries after his general health everybody responds, showing how deep his welfare lies in their hearts.

It is a touching thing to hear the tender inquiries framed by his daughters, and see how they hang, with rapt attention, on every word he says.

The morning greeting is invariably, from him, a fatherly kiss on the forehead, then he slides his arm around his daughter's waist, while the little questions that make up the sum total of home interest are asked and answered with a sweet gravity and seriousness that is perfectly charming to witness. Any playful badinage that may be indulged in only adds another charm to this sympathetic picture, and one can imagine how truly delightful it is to see a united family thoroughly "*en rapport*" with each other. Let me see, how many were we? First, there was the poet, and Mr. T. G. Appleton, Mr. and Mrs. Dana, Mr. Craig, Mr. Nathan Appleton, Miss Annie Longfellow, Miss Hale, myself and baby. His carriage, at the farthest end of the piazza, was carefully tended by nurse, but seeing the company, he began a series of vigorous outcries, and intimated that he had been neglected far too long.

The poet arose and went quickly up to him. Master Richard knew who was coming, and commenced crowing lustily, one of those effronted juvenile invitations to be taken up and petted. The favored one was the professor, and when he neared the baby carriage the dear thing put up its soft white hands, and almost sprang into grandpapa's arms.

He, nothing loth, took him up with all a mother's gentleness, and held the dainty bundle close against his breast.

It was a beautiful sight to see the old poet cradling his grandchild in his arms. The tender flesh of the young, contrasting its softness with the mature coloring of the elder, with the diminutive fingers tearing in and out the sire's snowy beard, and the curling dark locks of baby, finer than gossamer or cobwebs, mingling their dainty treasure with the bard's silvered hair. This formed a picture too

touching to be unremarked. Every moment the
baby's deep eyes would discover some new wonder
in grandpa's face, and with persistent cooing the
little hands would travel up and down the poet's
features, as only such mites of hands could travel,
with infancy's royal prerogative of license, and right
of way. His face lit up with a beautiful smile,
while the dainty creature caressed him. Ah! how
much a baby can say without speaking—and Longfellow understood, in the finest sense of the word,
the smallest wish of the little fellow. He would not
let him go, and baby caroled on, happy, so happy,
and seemed as unwilling to depart as grandpa was to
have him. Finally Mrs. Dana came forward and
remonstrated, saying:

"Now, papa, you have been a dear baby tender,
but I know you have had enough, and he will tire
you out. Pray let me take him, or let nurse look
after him, you have held him *so* long," the last with
a piteous little accent.

The poet looked up gravely, saying:

"Why, Edith, when *you* were little, I used to

hold you hours and hours, and it never seemed too much. So it is with your baby. I keep him fast in my arms, and almost fancy it is you yourself, a little thing helpless as he, and claiming all of my attention. You know how I love babies. Now *do* let him stay."

Another tug at his beard by the child, a frantic juvenile dash, a crow, and peculiar shout of laughter, followed by various vigorous movements, quite decides mamma.

She is inexorable. Baby has to go, for she will not tire her papa out, and he, never thinking of himself, would hold him till midnight.

Longfellow sighed, and with infinite reluctance yielded up his beautiful grandson to the legitimate tutelage, and settling back into his chair, the old expression of quietness stole over his face.

The morning was already half finished, and baby's departure was the signal for a stir among us.

The poet took the initiative, and asked what everybody thought of doing.

Some would go yachting, others had visits, Miss

Annie quite counted on her daily one hour sea-bath, and wild horses would not keep Mr. T. G. Appleton *now* from painting on his pebbles.

At last some one asked the professor his plans for the day, and he said :

" I think madame," turning to me, " would like to see something of Nahant and our surrounding country. I had thought of showing her Lynn, and if agreeable, we can take this afternoon for the visit. There is a fresh breeze, and I, myself, would enjoy getting a breath of it, while the day is so fine."

Of course, anything proposed by the poet was received from the onset with perfect favor, and it was decided that Michael would have the victoria ready by two, sharp, when we were to start.

We then dispersed, the professor to his apartment over the terrace, Mr. Appleton to his pebbles, Mr. Dana to the city, one here, another there, until luncheon would again summon such as were visible to the repast that evidently tried even Webster's powers of definition.

CHAPTER X.

THE REAL STORY OF HYPERION.

"O, scorn me as thou wilt, still, still will I love thee; and thy name shall irradiate the gloom of my life, and make the waters of Oblivion smile! And the name was no longer Hermione, but was changed to Mary; and the student Hieronymus—is lying at your feet! O, gentle lady,

'I did hear you talk
Far above singing; after you were gone,
I grew acquainted with my heart, and searched
What stirred it so! Alas! I found it love.'"

HYPERION, end chap. VIII.

"Tell me, my soul, why art thou restless? Why dost thou look forward to the future with such strong desire? The present is thine,—and the past,—and the future shall be. O, that thou didst look forward to the great hereafter with half the longing wherewith thou longest for an earthly future,—which a few days at most will bring thee! To the meeting of the dead as to the meeting of the absent! Thou glorious Spirit-land! O, that I could behold thee as thou art,—the region of life, and light and love, and the dwelling-place of those beloved ones whose being has flowed onward,

[142]

like a silver clear stream into the solemn-sounding main, into the Ocean of Eternity."

HYPERION, chap. II., book III.

THE poet is in good health to all outward appearances, but he eats little, almost nothing, and at luncheon I dared remonstrate, as his breakfast had been one but in name. He smiled faintly and said:

"Most people have a famous appetite at the seashore, but I never had. I think that the very sight and sound of it constitute sufficient nourishment. I love the ocean, and my soul is filled with something infinitely more satisfactory than the bread and meat of daily life. I feel a sense of completeness when in sight and sound of it, that I realize nowhere on land. I never tire of its strong, healthful breezes, and life-giving properties. Then, too, I love to think that it does me good, in a moral sense, and you know that must in the end be also of great physical benefit."

"Dear master," said I quickly, "if the sea soothes you, it must be good, but I cannot imagine that morally you would need its influence."

The rare, irresistible smile that I had so often seen came across his lips, and he said,

"I should hate to wait until I positively *needed* its influence; but we are all mortal, and I love to take the good where I find it, and above all, not to flee any teaching that may come, whether of voice, mind or current. To me the sea hath 'a thousand tongues,' all speaking in praise of a higher power, and a life to come that touches the realms of the - infinite."

His speech almost saddened me, and observing it, he said quite gayly,

"You must not look so serious. We shall gaze at the ocean, on our way to Lynn, when it seems quite a different affair from the puissant monster that rages up and down whole continents, and I promise you not one 'of the thousand tongues' shall accost you unless you yourself first give the signal. I see that our equipage is ready, and if you like we will start at once."

The open victoria stood waiting, and the horses— magnificent black, spirited animals, gave a little

neigh of pleasure, as if proud of the honor of carry-
ing the great poet.

The day was heavenly, and never have I seen the
professor in better spirits, if I may except the
slight tone of sadness that occasionally overcast his
fine countenance. He was in perfect health, and
determined to make the best of such propitious
weather.

It seemed impossible to imagine him other than
a young man. His voice was strong and full, and
had a happy ring that expressed contentment and
success, and he spoke of even indifferent things in a
way that was really charming.

As we neared the sort of road bridge that con-
nects Lynn with Nahant, he ordered the coachman
to drive slowly, so that he could "take in more
fully," as he said, "the beautiful panorama that
stretched out before us."

And in truth it was beautiful.

To the right, a small basin gave the idea of an
inland lake rather than the sea, and an enormous
black rock in the center called "Egg Rock," dark-

7

ened the water for a mile around. To the left of the embankment the breakwater formed a sluggish pool filled with weeds, and floating bits of bark and wood, and this muddy pond gradually grew less dark, as the waters went out to the sea.

We looked to the right as the prettiest part of the picture, and, musing, the poet spoke,

"Do you see that in the very edge of this basin a thousand little eddies come and go, rush upon the sands, then recede with a merry chattering out into the great waters, and then, back again? Well! it was just in sight and sound of this place that I wrote my poems, 'The Secret of the Sea,' and 'Palingenesis.' Each time I pass, I realize all of the old fascination for the spot, I hear again in my ears the same voices, and see those little fiendish waves dance back and forth with their endless rhythm and mystic chant.

"Look —— does it not seem a trick, the cunning way with which those white waves get back and sparkle over the sands, and their merciless hissing voices, as the current takes them out again to the sea? I know them so well."

I followed his eye and voice, and indeed, I could appreciate just the feeling that he described.

They seemed like old friends that beckoned and nodded to him, and at the same time kept repeating their endless good-bye until the carriage took us further and further away from the spot.

As we neared Lynn, I felt more in confidence with the professor, and we began talking of things that we had seen abroad.

The poet discoursed delightfully on his travels, and as we drove through the shady avenues of the old town, his voice mingled itself with the cadence of the sea, and the soft murmur of the summer air, that came through the branches of the lindens, making a sort of Æolian music, that was in perfect harmony with the scene. I can see the grand old man now, reposing against the cushions of the carriage, with his fine, frank face glowing with a beautiful carnation, the shapely head thrown back, and the snowy hair, silky and soft as spun glass, lying against the back of the seat, and contrasting vividly with the somber hue of the upholstery.

Mantled in his cloak, that gracefully covered his sloping shoulders, he had a pose of consummate ease, and the while talked quite unreservedly, now and then turning to me with a sweet smile, and ever and anon folding or clasping his hands, that otherwise lay quite still and motionless in his lap.

He had never before been so friendly, and I longed to improve that occasion to make him speak of himself. I had no morbid curiosity to know the slightest intimate detail of his life, but merely wished to hear him describe, in his own rare way, something relating entirely to his early travels in Europe.

Fate favored me. Turning a corner brusquely, we came in sight of the sea and a bit of scenery that caused him to exclaim :

" That reminds me of Switzerland. Have you ever seen Interlachen ?"

" Yes," said I, eagerly, " but tell me about it. I would rather know what you think of it. Were you there—when, alone—and—" he interrupted me sadly.

"No, not alone, but with friends; Mr. Appleton and his party." Then he stopped.

"No half confession," said I, gayly. "I am sure you are thinking of something very important, for your face looks grave and older, and I hear a half sigh coming from beneath your cloak. Pray tell me all about it."

He looked up affectionately, and patted my hand, saying, at the time:

"I don't know why I should speak to you, you are such a child, and this was a long time ago, but— do you not know," hesitatingly, "Mr. Appleton was an old acquaintance, and he introduced me to the party I mentioned, that I saw at Interlachen. I suppose something irresistible drew me there, for I had been traveling in another direction, and did not intend going that way, but they insisted, and I followed where Fate or any enterprising spirit led."

"Yes," I interrupted, "but the party you met, confess, were they all gentlemen, no ladies?"

He looked up, gravely. "No," said he, "there

were some ladies: one was Mr. Appleton's sister," a pause, drawing in his breath, " my late wife."

His voice deepened in feeling, and I lamented my own stupidity.

" Pardon me, dear master," I said, hesitatingly. " I did not know—I could not have imagined that I was nearing such a subject. I am sure you will never forgive me."

" There is nothing to forgive," said he, quietly. " To-day I am filled with memories of the past, and I am glad to talk with you, who seem to appreciate my feeble efforts to entertain you." Assuring me that " it did him good to speak," he continued, telling all about his travels; he said: " I went to Interlachen very heavy-hearted, and left it in almost the same state of sadness." Stopping suddenly he said: " But I am telling you all this. Have you never read Hyperion ?"

I confessed that I had, but so long ago that I remembered it only faintly. He looked at me curiously, and said, with some satisfaction and a half sigh :

" That is well, for the real ending was different, as you will now know. After the death of my wife in Rotterdam, I left Holland and traveled all over the Continent. In Switzerland I met the Appletons, who were voyaging for pleasure. Mr. Appleton, my wife's father, was very amiable. We were going to walk over the mountains, but he said : ' Why should you ? There is one seat in our carriage, and that is at Mr. Longfellow's disposal.' He turned to me with so hospitable a manner that I immediately accepted his invitation and sat *vis-a-vis* to Miss Fanny Appleton. They were so delicate and kind towards me that my heart warmed instinctively, and in their society one had little time for sad hearts and faces. The rest," said he, sweetly, " you know."

Not content with what the poet had said, I went still further and begged to ask him a question.

He considered, and said, " that if it were not too dreadful " he would answer it with pleasure ; at the same time he had anything but an unamiable look.

Remembering that he had been twice married, I asked him if he believed in affinities, and if he had

any warning or idea when he met Miss Appleton
that she would ever be his wife? I said, "Did you
love her at first sight?"

He started, as if of all questions that was the one
he least expected to hear, yet said to me with quiet
feeling and simplicity:

"You have asked—I will answer. Love comes
in various forms. I had no thought, then, that she
was other than a lovable and lovely woman, and it
was only some years afterward that I knew she was
all my world, and I began to hope for that which
Heaven after granted me. After our second meeting
we corresponded, and later she consented to take me
for her husband.

"No," he continued, "Fate is sometimes so un-
kind to let us not even *dream* of a happiness that is
in store. Could I have realized then, that the future
held one gleam of brightness, I think it would have
altered my character in many respects. Still, my
bitter complainings were all before my visit to Interlachen, and since then——"

"Since then," I repeated, with hushed voice,

"you have been blessed beyond the lot of ordinary mortals, and it has been also your good fortune to help to make others happy in the world, which is a rare joy, and one for which Heaven had selected you, as her special and gifted servant." His face glowed with a sublime faith, and he said with simple reverence :

"Yes, God is good !"

Back through the hushed town, back by the stirring trees and murmuring ocean, we retraced our way. The poet, after his long conversation, taken up, of course, at different intervals, kept very quiet until we reached home; and seeing him wrapped in thoughts of the past, nothing could have induced me to break the stillness of his musings.

His fair, aristocratic face outvied the tranquillity of nature in its repose, and over the calm features was drawn a fine vail of melancholy that sat upon his countenance like the mist that partially conceals the dawn, and hid this wonderful nature, that was sacred in its communion with memories of the past.

Before sleeping I re-read "Hyperion," and many

7*

things that had seemed sad and strange in the professor, were explained in the experience of Paul
Flemming. The book is really a history of his own
life, and his ideal woman, that in the last chapter he
bids adieu to forever as Fanny Asburton, became in
after years Mrs. Longfellow, *née* Fanny Appleton.

CHAPTER XI.

LONGFELLOW'S LOVE OF FLOWERS.

" In all places then, and in all seasons
    Flowers expand, flowers expand their light and soul-
        like wings,
    Teaching us by most persuasive reasons,
    How akin they are to human things."
                    FLOWERS.

" ' My Lord has need of these flow'rets gay,'
    The reaper said, and smiled;
   ' Dear tokens of the earth are they,
    Where he was once a child.

" ' They shall all bloom in fields of light
    Transplanted by my care,
    And saints, upon their garments white
    These sacred blossoms wear.' "
          THE REAPER AND THE FLOWERS.

LONGFELLOW is very fond of flowers.
Besides the garden's generous contribu-
tion, there are quantities sent to the poet
by admiring friends, and the house is
never without them. He loves them all, from the

tiny flow'ret that blooms modestly by the wayside, to
the gorgeous blossom that commands the attention
usually paid the pretentious. Mr. Longfellow pre-
fers violets, roses and lilies, although he rarely passes
a flower-bed, or a dainty thing growing among the
grasses, but he stops affectionately and plucks some
leaf or bud.

I remember last Spring, at Cambridge, a stroll
we took up and down the old walk. The trees, dis-
mantled of their snowy winter burden, were already
many-leaved, and the lawn had a velvety appearance.
The whole front of the garden facing Brattle street
has a thick hedge. or wall of bushes. These were
all in bud, and on the oldest branch there was one
spray of white lilac in full blossom. The poet
uttered an exclamation of pleasure as he saw it, and
with native gallantry plucked it and gave it me.

"You must keep it," said he naively, "'tis the
first one this season. I love Spring flowers, and I
particularly love the old-fashioned lilacs, yet they
make me sad."

His was an impressionable nature, and when

with his friends, he gave unrestrained utterance to
his thoughts. He was unusually quiet that morning,
and I said,

"*Cher maître*, why do these early flowers sadden you?"

He looked at me earnestly, and said,

"Whenever I take up one I ask myself, 'Will I
live to see another Spring-time?' I have a strange
idea, that if they welcome me with their first smile
I shall not die that year, but live just in sight of
another May. Promise me," this eagerly, "that
when I am gone you will place a branch of these
lilacs on my grave. Flowers are my oldest friends."
I was too touched not to promise as he wished, but
I scolded him playfully for his sad thoughts, and
refused to encourage such melancholy. To-day he
had the old look when he saw the fresh flowers in
the room, and at the first sign of sadness, I said
gayly,

"Dear master, *pas de tristesse*, these are not
lilacs." Before he could answer Mr. Nathan came
in with a mysteriously-covered parcel. A faint

something gleaming from under the fine tissue paper, suggested a bouquet or cut blossoms. Imagine what they were? Pink pond lilies, not the white or " yellow water lily," spoken of in Hiawatha, but the veritable flower in pink. I think I never saw anything so beautiful, and my astonishment was as great as my admiration. Professor Longfellow was more enthusiastic over them than any one, and he expressed himself in the warmest terms. Mr. Nathan explained that they had been brought originally from South Africa by a sea-captain, and transplanted near Sandwich, Cape Cod. They grew up almost white, but of late, with care, they have deepened into a lovely rose-pink. Strange to say, they are side by side with the white lilies, and never have propagated with them. They remain beautifully and distinctly pink, and each year become more lovely.

" They are not luxuriant," said Mr. Appleton, "and are found only in this one pond near Boston. It is a pity they are so scarce, as they would speedily become the ' *grand mode.*' "

"They are exquisite enough," responded Mr. Longfellow, "to become the fashion—they are inspiring, and these are particularly lovely." Mr. Nathan interrupted :

"They inspired Miss Jewett. She wrote a beautiful poem about them. Perhaps," turning to me, " you will also express your feelings in verse."

"But I never write poetry"—I objected.

"Never mind," said Mr. Nathan, " I dare you to this time. Every lady that sees these flowers protests an immediate inspiration, and you surely must try your hand."

Mr. Longfellow was quite interested and looked anxiously on, but I expostulated.

"I assure you I——"

"No," said Mr. Nathan, "I dare you. You must do it."

"I cannot ignore a dare," said I hastily, "but poetry—it seems dreadful to dash off anything in that fashion."

Mr. Longfellow interposed. "Try," said he ;

adding, amusedly, " you know a great deal of poetry is made to order ; why should you not succeed?"

" Very well," said I, " but give me a flower ; I cannot write without that."   Mr. Nathan gravely handed me the lily—the poet smiled good-humoredly, and said, " courage," while I withdrew to the little library. Three-quarters of an hour later I came out with a faded blossom but a flushed face.   In my hand was the following :

A PINK POND LILY.

1.

From far Ngami's golden shore
A gallant captain, passing o'er
  The river long and wide,
In a lonesome pool beyond the bank,
Mid waters dark and sea-weed dank
  A blushing flower espied.

2.

Then far from Afric's fevered smile
The lily fair did he beguile,
  And root and branch uptore.
He bore it in his ship of state
To newer land, to newer fate,
  Upon Cape Cod's lone shore.

3.

The flower drooped in its stranger bed,
Fretted, and drooped, and hung its head,
   To weep by day and night:
And when it reached Columbia fair,
To find itself transplanted there,
   Its color fled—'twas white.

  *   *   *   *   *   *   *

4.

O pallid flower, with petals cold,
O lovely form, with heart of gold,
   Mine, mine thou art in truth;
With wealth of sadness in thy face,
Each leaf of white symbolic grace,
   Fair emblem of our youth.

5.

As by the quiet meadow-side
A mirrored lake thy form doth hide
   A world of love unsought,
So with thy comrades to and fro,
The night-winds proud to thee shall blow
   The charm with which they're fraught.

6.

At last, with earthly care oppressed
The shades of evening bid thee rest,
   A pale, unworldly elf.
The soft caress, love's wayward charm,
Can ne'er to thee bring blight or harm,
   Thou'rt love and life thyself.

7.

And when the waters grieving loud,
With shadows dark and mist o'ercrowd
    Thy tender drooping crest,
So night's great privilege will show
To thee as to all flowers below
    Oblivion, peace, and rest.

8.

But shall thy head in death be bowed
Whose wealth of beauty, pure and proud,
    A crown of life desires.
Thou liest to-night in pallid bier,
Nor think'st to find enflaméd here
    Proud resurrection's fires.

9.

A broken heart doth sadly sleep,
The secret all the lilies keep,
    The secret of thy flight;
And then with bated breath they fold
Thy petals white, thy heart of gold
    Wrapp'd in the cloak of night.

10.

Yet hark.   Alectryon's trump doth call,
Aurora's lights rose-tinted fall
    On morning's dawn, then sink.
The stranger lily, once so white
Comes blushing from her buried night
    Comes forth with petals pink.

11.

And so the legend now is told,
About a flower with heart of gold
   That did her name forswear;
And said "adieu" to robes of snow,
With borrowed light to bloom and glow,
   A pink pond lily rare.

Nahant, July, 1880.

I gave up the poem. Mr. Longfellow with astonishment took it from me, and scanning it over, said quickly :

" The fourth and fifth verses are as good poetry as most can write, but the rest—I"—hesitating—"you must not feel badly, but I should scarcely call this a poem. It is a poetic sketch, and something might be made of it. Let me have it and I will correct it, and show you where and why the changes are made."

Mr. Nathan looked up quickly and said, " Two ladies have written on the same flower with totally different ideas. Who would have believed it ? Now the next person I dare "—

" Nathan," hastily interrupted the poet, " I don't think you had better ' dare ' any one else to write poetry, although "—checking himself adroitly, " had you not done so, we would have missed madame's lines."

"Oh! I know what you were going to say," I spoke up quickly. "But forgive me, I promise never to do so any more."

The poet looked happy again.

"That is right," said he honestly, "I think there are other things that you can do better than to write poetry, although I shall correct this if you wish, and if you still insist on making verses, I shall be glad to help you any way in my power."

Those were my first and last lines made to order, but I let Mr. Longfellow correct my sketch to keep as a souvenir of a pink pond lily.

CHAPTER XII.

LONGFELLOW IN CONVERSATION.

" Steadfast, serene, immovable, the same
 Year after year, through all the silent night,
 Burns on forevermore that quenchless flame,
 Shines on that unextinguishable light."

THE LIGHTHOUSE.

" Nothing useless is, or low;
 Each thing in its place is best;
 And what seems but idle show
 Strengthens and supports the rest."

RESIGNATION.

CALLS begin before luncheon, and the professor is always the recipient of several each day. Here the visitors are usually old friends, or recent agreeable acquaintances, instead of the crowd of curious, and autograph seekers that hunt out the Craigie mansion, and be-

tray themselves to the passers-by, in the shady
avenues of Cambridge.

Strange to say, the conversation rarely turns on
the subject of poetry.

Longfellow rarely argues. When he speaks, a
fine sensibility marks his demeanor, and a certain
self-respect that immediately gives dignity to the
topic under discussion, and commands the instant
attention of all present. The graces of his mind are
such that every sentiment receives just appreciation,
and before the thought finds expression his lips have
already framed an admirable and appropriate speech.

His language is strong, penetrating and beautiful,
rarely flowery, and devoid of useless words and re-
dundant adjectives. Senseless phrases are never
interlarded.

He says the wittiest things without intention, and
never stops to make a point in the midst of his
speech. In things that need real condemnation his
words are steel-pointed, and no barbed arrow ever
went nearer the mark. He speaks with conviction,
earnestness, and a certain eloquence as original as

fascinating. Whatever the subject, he attacks it boldly, honestly.

He employs no petty subterfuges of language to hide a real meaning. There are no fine speeches that cover a bad thought, or address themselves to what the world calls clever people. In politics, religion, civil reform or the fine arts, he is equally at home in understanding and discussion. How in the world Longfellow finds time to make himself master of all subjects, is simply puzzling. He needs only to read to remember, but it seems to me that twenty-four hours' study a day for a life-time would never have sufficed to acquaint him with all he knows, without this special intuitive gift of understanding.

He does not need to turn a subject over in his mind many times, before a just conclusion is arrived at.

This superhuman mental quality is rare to-day, and enjoyed, I think, in the highest sense by our great poet. It is not a question of being able to talk understandingly on general subjects, nor to criticise indiscriminately on every occasion, but to fabricate, from proper material, the structure that will best hold your ideas and thoughts. It is easy to tear down, but difficult to build. Longfellow, like Leonardo da Vinci, is an architect of the soul, and the solid foundation laid by nature has received additional pillars of thought and education, and plans of self-sustaining power, that show forth, in their completeness, the overwhelming beauty of truth, and truthful culture in man.

I doubt not that he could improvise, and the most noted of his lyrics show that beneath the shadow of the muse his heart has poured itself out in suddenly-inspired song, yet his speech has little of improvisation. It is more like the rounded utterance of one who has studied a subject deeply, and turned it over and over again in his mind.

My attention was called to this fact from observations made by his own family.

At the conclusion of some of his remarks I have frequently heard one of his daughters say :

" Why, papa, how funny. I never heard you express yourself on that subject before, and certainly not with such precision, and positive conviction; you have been studying it up to surprise us."

Then the poet would start hastily, and with utter gravity and modesty disclaim all special study of the question, remarking, simply:

" Have I not spoken of it before ? Well, that is not strange—although of course I have thought about it often ; still, not being an ordinary topic, it has been but little in my way."

On many questions the poet retains an obstinate silence. In vain does one try to draw him out. He listens with exquisite attention, but is cold, impassive and unyielding. No artifice of the calculating speaker can win from him the slightest sign of either approbation or disapproval. His manner is so positive that one must needs be hardy indeed to ask his opinion when he does not venture a word.

It is a great art to listen well—greater than that of speaking well. To those who have frequented men of letters and geniuses, it is refreshing to find a person who has no predilections in conversation, no

8

hobbies to discuss, and who does not harp continually on one subject.

I am not saying that Longfellow may not have one thought that is paramount to all others, and one ambition that the world knows has been gratified to its full. Poetry ever will be the god of his idolatry. A person not knowing him would at once allow him to be a man of culture, although they would be at a loss from his speech to know in what particular line his talents lay.

Whenever the conversation turns upon himself, as very often happens, he deftly draws attention to something else, but in a delicate way. Before one is aware, the subject gradually becomes less personal, and Longfellow directly appears pleased.

He takes real and unaffected interest in the pursuits of those who visit him, and when young people speak of what they are attempting to do in life, he questions them kindly and judiciously, never failing to encourage the fighter of life's battles to keep on in the good way.

One does not often hear from his lips sweeping

denunciations of religions, sects, societies, or any profession. If there be good in them, he is the first to speak of it, and if there be glaring faults, he tries to find an excuse, and expresses a hope for their future improvement and well-being.

A man possessed of Longfellow's keen insight into human nature cannot ignore the fact that while much is beautiful, much, alas! is morally very ugly in the world. The outward sign may be all that is tempting, like those lovely flowers that grow in far-off lands, where creeping waters hide their roots, and a deadly poison is exhaled from their petals, instead of the rare perfume that one expects from an enchanting exterior.

Because it exists and is bad, he would not uproot every vestige of the plant, but rather, like Father Lawrence, would seek to find the good, although to man still unrevealed.

The snows of many winters have silvered his hair, and he has had a great experience in life, yet withal, in face of his enormous instruction and still greater appreciation of the world, Longfellow is an optimist in the fullest sense of the word.

Perhaps it is this love of truth, and enjoyment of truthful things, that has in so great a measure shaped his life, and rendered him the most simple and unaffected of men; while at the same time he is more sensitive than another, and peculiarly alive to the coming in contact of an inharmonious nature.

I have felt when he was so tried. Without saying anything, one could see at once that some antagonistic element had forced its presence upon him, and he received at the same moment an instantaneous shock. He shivers mentally, and reminds one of a sensitive plant that, taken from its natural surroundings, is transplanted to the wayside, and feels for the first time the chill, piercing blast, and cold discomfort of an uncongenial clime. I sometimes think so impressionable a nature a doubtful gift.

Longfellow would have graced any century with his virtues, and even the " L'aureo trecento " (Golden Age) with his talent.

Of the three great poets who are claimed by the

Century of Gold, Petrarch was, perhaps, the most strictly virtuous, Dante the most impetuous, and Boccaccio the most careless of the trio. Longfellow resembles them only in his rare gift of natural song, and will hand down to history's page the record of a pure and stainless life.

Dante was reckless and lived a life of turmoil. The only pure affection he ever knew was the love of Beatrice, and that came to him when he had learned the value of a woman's smile. Boccaccio was vain, careless, but supremely gifted. Longfellow, on the contrary, has no vices, and lives out his exemplary life in the fear of God, beloved by man, and with exceeding tranquillity of mien. The world is better that he has lived in it.

CHAPTER XIII.

THE ORIGIN OF FISH CHOWDER.

" To whom the student answered: Yes;
   All praise and honor! I confess
   That bread and ale, home-baked, home-brewed,
   Are wholesome and nutritious food."

" Forthwith there was prepared a grand repast."

" Then her two barn-yard fowls, her best and last,
   Were put to death at her express desire,
   And served up with a salad in a bowl,
   And flasks of country wine to crown the whole."

THE MONK OF CASTLE MAGGIORE.—
TALES OF A WAYSIDE INN.

SOMEHOW to-day I feel quite strange, and alone. "Allons," I am already late. The sun has already covered everything outside with a golden glow, and to be in the house at such a time is criminal. Donning a dress of soft white cashmere, trimmed with lace and fringe, I prepare to descend, and stop once again to look in the glass. Reflectively, I say to myself, "White *is* becoming to blondes," and feeling already a little better in my mind, I join the family, who are loitering, as usual, on the back terrace.

"Why," said Mrs. Dana, quickly, "you look like a bride. What is it?"

"This is the anniversary of my wedding," said I, "and the first time that I have been alone on such a memorable occasion. But my husband must be '*en route*' for America; he expected to sail about this date, and news must soon come."

While I was yet talking, a servant brought me a dispatch. Thanks to Cyrus Field's Atlantic cable, one can talk across continents, and I read "Sail to-day in 'Gallia,' all well, love." This had been sent from Liverpool, and already my husband was on his way. The professor smiled pleasantly, and all wished him the safest of voyages.

We talked on of different things and brought up the subject of the Boston Cadets, and a recent pleasant visit to the camp. The commanding officer, Colonel Hayes, was very polite, and we had an opportunity of seeing the "boys" near by as they came up from their splendid drill, and passed in front of the colonel's tent.

The time passed away so quickly that it was late before we had even thought of leaving, and then, accompanied by the charming Miss Sarah Jewett and Miss Hayes, the colonel's sister, we finally left the pleasant green to go to Nahant proper, or rather to the poet's house, as we were all to dine with him.

When we returned, he was loud in his praise of the cadets, and regretted that a slight cold had kept him in doors. You see, it was rather risky going so far, and being obliged to keep one's feet all of the time upon the wet ground, so soon after recent rain ; and the professor was very wise not to think of it. We sat down to-day, a jolly party, and I must say here, that one does not often get such dinners outside Paris. Every day we had fish chowder by request, but this evening there was a change.

When the table was all ready and the guests were seated, Mr. T. G. Appleton raised his head and explained,

"To night our chowder is different; instead of fish —— "

"It is clam," interrupted the professor, with a grim little smile.

"How did you know?" said his brother-in-law quickly.

"I did not know," said Longfellow; "I only saw that you looked as if you were about to announce a matter of great moment, and by your partially designating the dish, I thought it referred to a change in our favorite soup. Although not radical, it is a change. Chowder is always chowder, but *fish* chowder is never clam."

"I cannot understand," I broke in, "what it all means; what is chowder, how is it made, and what language does it speak? who will tell me about it?"

Mr. T. G. Appleton looked up, and during the pauses of helping his hungry guests, he said:

"I will explain, and gladly." Even the professor looked interested, and Mr. Appleton began.

Stop, before he speaks I must describe him. He has a portly form, tall, and well furnished. His eyes are steady, dark, and they burn with a look at times that must be agony to the conscious man, for he certainly will get everything out of him, no matter how much he might want to conceal. His face is strongly marked, with heavy brows, thick mustache, and an expression of such rare intelligence that an Italian after saying "astuzia" would give it up, for "astuzia" means shrewdness, and our amiable host, besides possessing that quality, adds to it a world of natural wit and talent, aided by the most advantageous study of human nature that wide travel and a liberal education could possibly afford. Besides being a charming man in every way, he is kindliness itself, and the best story-teller one ever listened to. Whatever he talks about his way of putting it is refreshing, delightful, and altogether palatable.

The professor looked brightly wide awake, and in answer to my asking "What is chowder?" Mr. Appleton began.

"Chowder,"—he glances around—everybody is listening.

"Chowder," he repeats, daintily ladling out the savory soup, "is only good when made in private houses. At hotels it is watery and insipid, while the fish and chowder crackers are usually boiled to rags. The way to make it is this. The fish (cod or haddock) should be broken into large flakes, and boiled twenty minutes with plenty of salt pork and milk and chowder biscuits. The dish was probably obtained by New England fishermen from the French, who for two centuries have been catching and salting the cod, which is also immensely used in countries bordering on the Mediterranean. When salted it is called '*baccalao*.' The New England fishermen told their wives of this good and simple dish, and taught them how to make it. The women asked what it was called, and in reply were told that they had heard a good deal of a word like 'chowder.' The real word they had heard was *chaudière*, not the thing itself, but the kettle in which it was cooked."

Mr. Appleton looked around.

This was the real reason, undoubtedly, why

chowder was called chowder, and I was very glad to know the origin of the dish.

In the midst of the talking and pleasant click of the champagne glasses the professor arose, and lifting his, said with grave ceremony, and tender grace,

"'Les absents ont toujours tort' (the absent are always in the wrong), according to the French proverb, but to-day I beg an exception to the general rule in favor of my young friend, Signor Macchetta. This is the anniversary of his wedding day, and although he may not hear, I propose his life-long health and happiness, and that of my young guest, Madame, his wife. May he have a prosperous voyage, and may the good ship 'Gallia' bring back to our hospitable shores the loving husband and ever-welcome friend."

Then there were shouts and happy speeches, congratulations without number, and of course, I was quite a heroine. One could not help feeling touched at the dear old poet's attention, and I noticed for the first time that the table was more than usually handsome. Lovely flowers here and there covered the fine damask cloth, and some way the dinner partook more of a fête than an every-day affair. It had been so delicately managed, that I, least of all, was suspicious of what was going to happen when Professor Longfellow got up, but now that it was done, and done with such grace, who would not have felt honored and proud to have such a thoughtful friend ? All joined with equal good-will and sympathy in trying to make my anniversary a happy one.

The night was so still that during the dinner we heard the first sound of the bells of Lynn borne across the waters, and I called to mind the poet's beautiful lines :

"Oh, curfew of the setting sun! O Bells of Lynn!
Oh, requiem of the dying day! O Bells of Lynn!

From the dark belfries of yon cloud, cathedral wafted,
Your sounds aerial seem to float, O Bells of Lynn!

Borne on the evening wind across the crimson twilight,
O'er land and sea they rise and fall, O Bells of Lynn!

The fisherman in his boat, far out beyond the headland,
Listens and leisurely rows ashore, O Bells of Lynn.

Over the shining sands the wandering cattle homeward
Follow each other at your call, O Bells of Lynn!

The distant light-house hears, and with his flaming signal,
Answers you, passing the watchword on, O Bells of Lynn!

And down the darkening coast run the tumultuous surges,
And clap their hands and shout to you, O Bells of Lynn !

Till from the shuddering sea, with your wild incantations,
Ye summon up the spectral moon, O Bells of Lynn!

And startled at the sight, like the weird woman of Endor,
Ye cry aloud and then are still, O Bells of Lynn!"

CHAPTER XIV.

LONGFELLOW'S LOVE OF MUSIC.

"And the night shall be filled with music,
And the cares that infest the day
Shall fold their tents like the Arabs,
And silently steal away."

THE DAY IS DONE.

E passed the evening delightfully, and some near neighbors and friends coming in, the current of conversation was led into various channels. The poet is passionately fond of music, and Mr. Haines, a cultivated amateur, played and sang some charming selections. I also had the honor of singing, at the poet's request, the famous prayer from Rossini's Otello, sung by Desdemona in the finale of the great scene, "*Assisa a pié d'un salice.*"

[183]

The prayer has no variations, with the exception of a few changes at the end, written by Malibran, and so admired by Rossini himself that they have become traditional.

Longfellow listened with tears in his eyes.

"Pray sing it again," said he, eagerly, when I had finished; "those few notes to me contain more real heart-felt music than anything that Rossini ever wrote. How well I can picture to myself the anguished Desdemona under the influence of some terrible impending calamity, praying Heaven with all her heart to give her peace and rest. How touching the words." Then slowly to himself he repeated, in a voice deep with suppressed feeling:

> "Deh! calma o ciel, nel seno
> Per poco le mie pene—
> Fate che l'amto bene
> Me vengo a consolar."

> (Ah, calm, O Heaven, in my sad breast
> For e'en a while this grief.
> Come, spouse beloved, although brief
> Thy stay. It consolation brings.)

There was silence for a moment following his

words, and the faint chords of the prelude recom-
mencing, his request was complied with. After that
there was no more music. The night was still and
soft, and we all adjourned to the terrace overlooking
the sea.

The poet, enveloped in his long cloak, sat in an
arm-chair facing the water, and I looked at him
almost expecting to see a saint's halo descend upon
his head. The moon was high in the heavens, and
the firmament glittered with its myriad of stars. A
breeze, unusually soft for night, fluttered gently in
and out, stirring the almost tropical verdure at Nahant
with a faint rustle. The sea, like a fountain overrun
with liquid silver, swept its long train of heaven-
lighted waves back and forth upon the strand, up
and down the little beach, and yet out again to the
middle of the water lying between Nahant and
Lynn.

Mr. Appleton's yacht, the pretty "Alice," lay
out from the shore. Mr. Longfellow was very fond
of her. She crossed the Atlantic in 1866; but
to-night, bathed in moonlight, she made a white

speck on the wave, and seemed more a phantom than a real sloop. Her dainty mast leaned so timidly against the sky that even the shadow was unearthly. One half expected it to appear and disappear as did Heinrich Hudson's, the night that poor Rip Van Winkle entered upon his twenty years' sleep.

The poet sat and gazed upon the sea, upon the moon, upon the stars, and the while his face shone with a heavenly brightness that completely illumined it. The rays from the majestic orb silvered anew his snowy hair, crept cunningly in and out of his beard, and danced over his vesture with elf-like grace, and inimitable friendliness.

They seemed to say, " You belong to us—you are not of earth, but part of a heavenly body in the great plan of Nature, given for the world's benefit; and so to-night we come to greet you with affectionate love and the kindred message which emanates from souls that only haunt the earth but belong really to a higher power. Thus the Queen of Night sends greetings to the King of Poetry."

They flickered on, brighter and stronger, until

his form gleamed with light and his face looked like that of one of the saints of old receiving the heavenly benédiction. The fire of his soul glittered in his blue eyes, like sapphires when the sun shines on them.

He sat there in his old age, a patriarch whom not only the smiles of day but of night shone upon—loved by all the world and revered by those who could know the innate purity and tranquillity of his home life, with the mantle of a fame fallen upon his shoulder, whose warmth outshone Hæphestus' fires, and cloaked him with a dignity and immortality that the world has rarely seen.

Long he sat musing, and no one disturbed his revery. Miss Annie had been swinging in her hammock, but finally got up and went with some of the party a bit of the way from the house, to a famous ravine or drift in the rocks, which, when the moon shone down upon it, was said to be surpassingly lovely.

Not caring for a nearer view than could be had from the balcony, I did not go, but remained beside the poet—who, while quiet and melancholy, was not so silent as heretofore. He spoke with more than his accustomed gentleness of voice, but I could see that he was in no mood for conversation ; nor did he care to be alone — he simply seemed permeated with a great sense of quietness and calm, and his body showed the utter restfulness of his soul by its immovability and statue-like repose.

While we were sitting, each one wrapped in thought, a burst of music rang out on the air, and the sounds came from some distance, borne directly by the wind towards the house.

A regiment of Boston militia had been camping out at Nahant for some time, and every evening they held a sort of reception after their drill. Evidently the day's ceremonies were ended, and this was the "home march for everybody."

The poet looked up quickly and lent a listening ear. Again I noticed in his face the same expression as when listening to the "Otello," and he said :

"What can be more delightful than sounds of melody wafted to one from some mysterious source !

When night has fallen, and the sights and sounds of daily strife are hushed by the murmur of the winds among the leaves and the crash of the breakers against the shore, all nature seems in harmony with man, and it only needs the added charm of that distant music to complete the beauty of this evening."

"I have a favor to ask, dear master," said I, interrupting him. "Will you not recite to me your poem of——"

"The Day is Done?" said he, interrupting me sadly. "Certainly, if it will give you pleasure. I mention 'The Day is Done,' because I know you must have referred to that."

He then commenced the first stanza and recited until the end with a clear, sweet voice, exquisitely modulated, and a depth of earnestness in his tones which no one in the world could have shown as well as he. I never tire of reading this poem, and say it over to myself so often that every word is stamped upon my memory. He began:

> "The day is done, and the darkness
> Falls from the wings of night,

As a feather is wafted downward,
  From an eagle in his flight.

" I see the lights of the village
  Gleam through the rain and the mist,
And a feeling of sadness comes o'er me
  That my soul cannot resist.

" A feeling of sadness and longing
  That is not akin to pain,
And resembles sorrow only
  As the mist resembles the rain.

" And the night shall be filled with music,
  And the cares that infest the day
Shall fold their tents like the Arabs,
  And silently steal away."

The last words died out to a faint murmur, but
the old poet's face still bore its inspired look.
Thanking him with deep feeling, I prepared to say
" good-night," as the air was getting a little chill,
and I feared keeping him any longer; also—may I
say it?—I wished to retire before the sound of any
other voice could disturb the lingering memory of
the professor's inspired tones. As I said " good-
night" he arose, and spoke with infinite tenderness :

"God bless you, ' *chere enfant*,' and may your
life be one of happiness and content; *dormez bien*,
and good-night."

He bowed with courtly grace, and led me through the still opened window back to the drawing-room. I left him, but, turning, I said:

"*Cher maître,* are you not thinking of soon taking your rest? This has been a long and tiresome day for you, I fear, although to me it has been so enjoyable."

I looked at his face, and it seemed older than usual, and I knew he must be tired, although he said:

"I cannot go just yet; besides, I think I hear voices, and I must see my daughter to say good-night. I could not sleep were I to retire now; again, *bonne nuit.*"

Sleep! I could not sleep myself, but lay thinking over the day's events for some time. Of the many great men whom it had been my fortune to meet, none, not one, could claim to be the man that Longfellow is. His is a soul that looks straight ahead, and while he must have known all the fascination that comes to the life of a public man, yet never, in the slightest way, did a too worldly sentiment

ever escape him, or a spoken thought, that was not
pure and wholesome, ever pass his lips. I felt that
this man was one among men, perhaps the only poet
whose inner life has been one beautiful hymn, and
whose daily intercourse with the world left not one
imprint on the stainless character, one mark by
which the fatal traces of passion and worldliness
could ever show themselves, other than in a lofty
sense. I could not help praying that one whose
influence was so grand and *puissant*, might defy, for
many years to come, the approach of the angel
whose visit leaves only desolation behind.

CHAPTER XV.

" A cold, uninterrupted rain,
  That washed each southern window-pane
  And made a river of the road;
  A sea of mist that overflowed
  The house, the barn, the gilded vane,
  And drowned the upland and the plain,
  Through which the oak-leaves broad and high
  Like phantom ships went drifting by."
                TALES OF A WAYSIDE INN, Part II.

" Not chance of birth or place has made us friends,
  Being oftentimes of different tongues and nations,
  But the endeavor for the self-same ends,
  With the same hopes, and fears, and aspirations."
                                DEDICATION.

OR two days the rain has kept us within
doors and I can scarcely say that I regret
it, as the poet has been indefatigable in
his efforts to keep us enlivened, and I
have had the rare treat of hearing him speak at

9   [193]

length on many subjects, more or less interesting. The hours passed under his roof have constituted the greatest intellectual event of my life-time. His beautiful ideas, and sweet way of expressing them, are filled with an ineffable charm, and his voice is in keeping with his poetic face and appearance.

I had a copy of " Les Travailleurs de la Mer " in my hand when I came down-stairs late in the afternoon, and the professor noticed it.

" I am glad to see you reading Victor Hugo," said he, amiably ; " he is a great poet and writer, and his works, besides possessing infinite charm and vigor, are really instructive. Of course his great forte is in his imaginative and descriptive power. He is grand and pathetic."

I interrupted :

" I know the old poet so well, that I read his writings with still more pleasure, however. His description of the devil-fish in this is so terribly graphic that I screamed out all alone by myself just an hour since, as if really in the clutches of this horrible monster. I think I have learned more of the wonders of the deep from this, than any other story I ever read. His imagination, as you say, is so extraordinary that one scarcely knows where to draw the line between it and reality."

Mr. Longfellow said quickly, "You know Victor Hugo? Pray tell me about him. Strange to say I never saw him but once, and then at a distance?"

I could not help smiling as the poet spoke, and he said, "Why do you smile?"

"You great writers," I answered readily, "all want to know about each other. The last time I was at his house he asked about you, using exactly the same words, but alas! not knowing you then personally, I could tell him nothing. On the contrary, I can tell you everything of him, if you care to hear."

"Tell me," said Longfellow, "what kind of a man he is, how he lives, and if it be true, as people say, that he sits on a throne in his own house?"

This last half laughingly.

"Prepare for a long recital," said I, jestingly, and began :

"Victor Hugo lived at No. 21 Rue de Clichy, in Paris, when I first knew him. Now he has removed to a fine house near the Arc du Triomphe in Avenue d'Eylau, I believe, named "Avenue Victor Hugo" in honor of the poet. He used to receive at his house every Thursday and Sunday evenings, and around him were gathered the principal literary lights of France. He does not 'sit upon a throne,' as many have said, but his arm-chair is so large and peculiar in shape, that devotees of the mansion have nicknamed it 'le trône du Maître,' and I suppose for all time it will retain its title.

"His dwelling-place was a very large apartment, with ample rooms. From the moment the door opened into the antechamber all was light and comfort. The walls of the reception and drawing-rooms were hung with Venetian tapestry in red and gold. Rich stripes of embroidered yellow satin alternated with ones of the same size in scarlet velvet. The ceiling was covered in the same way, and held in the center a superb chandelier of gold and rock crystal, glittering with a thousand lights furnished by innumerable waxen tapers. You know it is considered vulgar to use gas in a salon in Paris. All around the room were curiously-carved magnificent cabinets in renaissance and Venetian work. They were filled with medals and collections of coins, bric-a-brac, and valuable souvenirs, exquisite in taste and lavish in quantity.

" Strange to say, not a book was to be seen, nor was there a piano. Five immense oval mirrors (Venetian) hung around the room in various places, and the intervening panels of the principal apartment were hung with superb renaissance candelabra, some of them centuries old, and giving the apartment a very quaint Louis-the-Fourteenth look, and a real old-fashioned air. It is the sort of room one would expect to find Victor Hugo in. The furniture was of dark crimson velvet and rosewood. The windows, heavily-curtained, had portieres or hangings of the same material at the doors. There was a circular divan or dos-a-dos in the center of the room, and near the fire-place, the comfortable arm-chair that is called the master's throne.

" The poet is of medium height, and rather stout ; his hair and beard are quite gray, and while the one is ample, the other is very scant, his head being almost bald. He has a kind face, heavily furrowed, and rather sad. His smile is a pleasant one, and is the only beautiful thing about his countenance, which is often dark and troubled. His brow bears the impress of intense thought. His eyes are profound and steady: I cannot tell whether they are black or gray, but they seem nearer a brownish hazel than either, and are very expressive without being positively remarkable. He is a perfect gentleman of the old school, and receives his guests with French ceremony, not unmixed with a certain genial friendliness that is very frank and seemingly sincere.

" On the occasion of one visit to him I had the honor of crowning him with a laurel wreath on the anniversary of his seventy-third birth-day.

" By the way, maestro," turning to Longfellow, "he was born the twenty-sixth of February, and yourself the twenty-seventh of the same month, so you see that Calliope had you both in her mind about

the same time, although several years elapsed between."

Our poet interrupted.

"Never mind me," said he, smiling; "you cannot tell how interested I am to hear more of Victor
Hugo. What else happened that evening?"

"Several Americans in Paris," I continued, "who
had long enjoyed his hospitality and the charm of
his society, decided on presenting him with the
wreath and some flowers as a slight testimonial of
their remembrance.

"I was selected for the proud office of placing
the laurel on his honored head, also to read two original poems written for the occasion by Arsène Houssaye, the celebrated French novelist. I nearly killed
myself going up some rickety stairs—I don't know
how many—in the Palais Royale, to get M. Martel,
of the Théatre Française, to teach me how to recite
them properly.

"These are the lines, and, my French being per-
ilous in those days, I think I must have learned them
parrot-fashion, by dint of repeating them an hundred

times or more. The accent must have been, to say
the least, peculiar, and I wonder I ever dared try it.

"'TO VICTOR HUGO.

1.

" ' Ton génie est la cime aux eblouissements
  La nature sourit a tes apothéoses
  La vigne est la Fôret en leurs metamorphoses
  Se traduissent tes vers, et content tes romans.

2.

" ' Ton génie est la source ou boivent les amants
  Courrant par les jardins tout parfumé des roses
  S'enivrant du parfum des fleurs blanches et roses
  Et jetant a la mer, perles et diamants.

3.

" ' Ton génie est un ciel en sa beauté première
  Quand le jeune soleil rayonne épanoni
  Quand les étoiles d'or chantent l'hymn inoui.

4.

" ' Ton génie est un monde où Dieu met sa lumière
  Parceque ton esprit cherche la verité,
  Ton âme l'infini et ton cœur l'humanité.'

" Imagine after that the sensation. Victor Hugo
jumped up and embraced Arsène Houssaye, and
they kissed each other on both cheeks in real French

fashion. Everybody came forward to congratulate the author of the verses and the one to whom they were addressed ; the flowers were presented, and such well-known persons as Louis Blanc, Ernest de Hervilly, Richard Lesclide, Paul Le Roy, Theo. de Banneville, and a host of others, among whom was our American Minister, your friend Hon. E. B. Washburne, all crowded up to get a word with the poet. He having previously said that his anniversary was a sad day, 'triste jour,' and one that he spent in absolute solitude, we were obliged to celebrate the event the evening before, and Arsène Houssaye, anticipating his oft-reiterated words, had prepared still another poem, which I read, and which seems to me prettier even than the first.

"'ARSENE HOUSSAYE.

1.

"'Dimanche tu disais, ne chantons pas ma fête
Puisqu' une année encore m'approche du tombeau
L'amour passe a la mort le feu de son flambeau,
Le cypres est le seul bouquet qui ceint ma tête.

2.

" ' Tu ne crains pas la mort, sourde, aveugle et muette
  Ce n'est pas pour Hugo qui chante le corbeau
  Continue a chercher le vrai comme le beau
  Les hommes comme toi sont des Dieu, O Poët.

3.

" ' La jeunesse a trempie ton âme! Tu vivras
  Les siècles ne seront pour toi que des années
  Quand Dieu t'appellera vers d'autres destinées.

4.

" ' C'est l'immortalité qui t'ouvrira ses bras
  Toujours jeune et toujours belle c'est le mystère
  Tu seras chez les Dieux, mais sans quitter la terre.' "

" How beautiful," said Longfellow, when I had finished, " I do not wonder that he was pleased, what *did* he say ?"

" Say ——" I repeated. " He didn't *say* anything, but the tears came into his eyes and again he tendered his hand to the author, and they embraced each other as before, although this time they were visibly much moved; we spent a very delightful evening, and when the last person had dispersed the midnight bells were striking all over Paris. I used to spend every Thursday at his house, and usually

Sunday evenings. Monday was a special day, but I remember once when I was there, after spending a long time' in discussion, a little before ten, we went out to have some refreshment. He sat at the head of the table, with his dear old friend Madame Drouét his vis-a-vis. There were fourteen people present, and he made a charming host, talking now and then himself, drawing out the others, and all the while he was eating sliced oranges with great appetite, and drinking some fine old burgundy, to which he added three large lumps of sugar to each half-glass, stirring it vigorously, and then quaffing two-thirds of it at a single draught. I have seen him so many times, but remember also particularly one evening, when he commenced talking on art and the galleries in Holland and Belgium. It was a superb lecture, and he talked unremittingly for two hours. Every word that comes out of his mouth is a pearl of great price. I never in my life learned so much before of the Flemish school of painting, and his description of certain pictures was so perfect that on a subsequent visit to Holland I recognized

them from his describing, without the aid of guide
or catalogue.   He is a remarkable speaker, and oh!
so eloquent.   He is very simple in his manners, and
never before have I heard any one who could pay a
more delightful compliment than he.

" To the young poets who flock around him and
fill his rooms, he is especially amiable, and in speaking of his way of complimenting I refer more particularly to them, as he always found some delicate,
sweet thing to say just in the moment when it was
least expected, and there was a subtleness about his
remarks that was often very wonderful.

" Strange to say, he speaks of the time when he
was exiled as one might refer to a dinner, without
emotion, without sentiment, simply a recurrence to
fact.

" A great many titled people come to see him, in
fact, more noblemen than commoners, but no one is
called otherwise than simple " Monsieur." Victor
Hugo himself is always addressed as " Cher maître,"
by both ladies and gentlemen.   The latter sometimes
kiss his hand affectionately, if they be students or

young aspirants for literary honors, while Victor Hugo never kisses a lady's hand, but always her wrist.

" He certainly is original, and that to me is charming. His speech is soft and insinuating, and while any one else is talking he never takes his eyes from their face, but sits with his chin propped against his hand, the very picture of expectant curiosity and serious attention. He puts questions with great adroitness, and is as grave as a lawyer while awaiting a response.

" Although he lived so long a time at Guernsey, on the coast of England, he speaks but little English. But I am sure he knows the language as well as we, from the look on his face, when one speaks it. He always says, ' Oh, my son Charles spoke beautifully,' referring to English, and his knowledge of Shakespeare was remarkable. 'Pauvre Charles,' then he would sigh, and I do not wonder; the loss of such a man to the world of letters was something, but the loss of such a son was enough to sadden any father."

" By the way," said Longfellow, "he *did* know Shakespeare, because his translation of the English

bard's noted works is the most complete and faithful
to the text of any published in the French language.
It is paying him a truthful compliment to say that
his work will stand any amount of close reading and
criticism."

" François Charles Hugo, as he was called, left
two children, and these little ones are the delight of
Victor Hugo's life.   He is very fond of his daughter-
in-law, who has since married Mr. Henry Lockroy, of
the French Parliament, and he passes most of his
time with his beloved grandchildren, playing with
them quite alone.

"But how I am rambling on, dear master," said
I, turning to Longfellow, " and I have not yet told
you of what he said of your own poems."

Longfellow looked up sweetly.

" I cannot tell how interesting it has been," said
he ; " nor how much I wish that I had met him.
Pray go on."

" He knows your principal poems by heart, and
pronounces most of them beautifully ; and he seems
equally well acquainted with the text and subject

He calls you a 'heart-reader,' and referred to the sentiment and purity of your writings. He liked 'Hiawatha' particularly; but it was amusing to hear him pronounce the word. Excuse me, but it *was* a mouthful. He got on beautifully until he came to the *w* commencing the third syllable, when his mouth got into a twist, and poor 'watha' was strangled between a Dutch *v* and an Italian *a* that threatened to obliterate every vestige of the original sound of the letters. Of course I laughed, and everybody else appreciated the poet's peculiar pronunciation of English. As Victor Hugo good-naturedly smiled himself, his satellites knew that they could chime in with him, and everybody with a proper respect still seemed to enjoy his English immensely.

"He is very kind to Americans, and seems particularly pleased to receive them in his house. He longs to visit America, but I am afraid he never will. He calls this ' the country of wonders'—'*le pays des merveilles*'—and is really and genuinely enthusiastic when talking about it."

In speaking of his home life, I said that he spent

much time with his "little" grandchildren. I am afraid I must alter that statement, as they are no longer so "little," and he is now a Senator, so of course things are much changed. He is hale and hearty, and when he goes about he rides on the tops of omnibuses so that he can "study character," as he expresses it. No one clambers up with readier step than he, and he sometimes smokes a pipe with great stolidity of countenance, and looks around his dear Paris that he can never see too much of. He chats with his elbow-neighbor on the 'bus, whether prince or laborer, with the greatest friendliness imaginable, and when he gets down goes off with right good will, saluted reverentially by everybody around him. Not a working-man in his district but knows him, and his face is as familiar to the regular Parisian as the light of the sun or his own famous Notre Dame de Paris. He is really beloved by the people, and is vastly fond of talking of the "Model Republic—America," and the "Great Republic—France."

"When you see him," said Longfellow, with hearty sincerity, "present him my special compliments. If I ever go to Paris again I shall not fail to pay him a visit; and in the meantime do not forget to tell him how he is loved and appreciated in America, and how honored I shall be to shake him by the hand."

CHAPTER XVI.

SKETCHES DRAWN FROM LIFE.

"Around the fireside, at their ease,
   There sat a group of friends, entranced
   With the delicious melodies;
   Who from the far-off noisy town
   Had to the wayside inn come down,
   To rest beneath its old oak trees:
   The fire-light on their faces glanced,
   Their shadows on the wainscot danced,
   And, though of different lands and speech,
   Each had his tale to tell, and each
   Was anxious to be pleased, and please,
   And while the sweet musician plays,
   Let me in outline sketch them all,
   Perchance uncouthly, as the blaze
   With its uncertain touch portrays
   Their shadowy semblance on the wall.

" A young Sicilian, too, was there;
   In sight of Etna born and bred,
   Some breath of its volcanic air
   Was glowing in his heart and brain,

[210]

And being rebellious to his liege,
After Palermo's fatal siege,
Across the western seas he fled."

TALES OF A WAYSIDE INN.—PRELUDE.

OME months had passed since my Nahant visit when I went again to Cambridge. It was Christmas night, and besides Signor Monti, a great friend of the professor, my husband and myself were the only strangers present. The house was a beautiful picture in itself, and the hanging wreaths and garlands showed the presence of the holy natal tide. The poet was as usual extremely courteous and kind, and the evening passed with delightful charm. I recognized in Mr. Monti an old friend of the professor, and he said to me during the dinner:

" This is the *young* Sicilian that I have known so long, and love so well," looking as he spoke directly toward Mr. Monti with an affectionate smile.

Signor Monti was evidently gratified, and said, with ready grace, speaking our language perfectly:

" Yes, I am the once *young*, now *old* Sicilian

mentioned in ' The Tales of a Wayside Inn.'   Did you
not recognize me ?"

"Of course," said I heartily, "I ought to have
done so at once, but not thinking about it, my imagination has proven itself excessively torpid.   It never
entered my mind that you were the real 'Signor
Luigi' spoken to by the Jew; but," turning to Longfellow, " let me ask you a question.   Are all of the
characters bonâ fide in the poem, and may I know
who they are ?"

Longfellow looked up quite gayly, and said,

"Yes, I think you may, but Mr. Monti shall
answer.   Let him tell the story."

Mr. Monti would not hear to that, so Mr. Longfellow began to speak.   "Mr. Monti and his friends
used to steal away every summer for their vacation
to the little town of Sudbury, not far from Boston,
and they had such fine times among themselves, I
really thought that I should like to join their party
to pass my next summer.   They insisted on my coming, and I was so charmed with the place that I immediately conceived my poem, ' The Tales of a Way-

side Inn.' The house, although quaint and old-fashioned, was interesting in one way. Three pairs of lovers used to steal in and out of the old tavern, and three modest fiancées would regularly come to the trysting-place in the vine-embowered garden. Later on the same three couples were married in fine style, and took each other for better or worse. One was Monti and his wife, the other was the poet Theophilus Parsons, and the third couple was Dr. Parsons, sister and her fiancé.

" Ah! those were happy times. Why, do you know, Monti was so fond of the place, that he went there for twelve consecutive seasons, and I don't know but the others did the same, now that I think of it. I went a number of times until the inn fell into disuse, and after my poem was finished, it was strange to say, almost abandoned by our old party. Still it was a charming spot, and so home-like. The old inn is standing now, although sadly changed, and I fear that of the number who once passed so many happy hours there, not one to-day would think of returning unless by way of a souvenir for Auld Lang Syne."

"But the other characters," I interrupted, "who were they? did they *really* exist?"

"Really," said the poet, laughing; "why, *of course.* Professor Daniel Treadwell was the Theologian; Henry Wales, Esq., was the Student; Lyman Howe was the Landlord, and our Italian friend here before you was and is Luigi Monti, the Sicilian."

"The only fictitious character," interrupted the Signor, "was the Jew. That is Mr. Longfellow's secret, he will never tell who he was; but you have forgotten to say that the musician was Ole Bull," continued Mr. Monti. "I am sure madame must often have heard him play."

"Who," said I quickly, "has not heard of the 'Wizard of the North'? and what American but has listened to his playing? I knew him well. He was a charming gentleman, besides being a good story-teller—and such an amiable man, while the whole world acknowledged his wondrous talent."

Mr. Monti evidently did not intend letting the

professor off about the unknown character in the
"Tales of a Wayside Inn."   Turning to him, he said,
with Italian perverseness :

"Confess the Jew was ——" The poet, with a
cunning smile, broke in :

> " 'A Spanish Jew from Alicant,
>   With aspect grand and grave was there ;
>   Vendor of silks and fabrics rare,
> And attar of rose from the Levant.'

I am sure," continuing helplessly, "I could not
describe him better than that.   Are you satisfied ?"

Monti laughed heartily, and gave in that the
Professor was altogether too clever for him.   He
would give up trying to find out who he was.   But,
he added, with a characteristic gesture, to me, later :

"Many have wondered who the Jew was, and
between ouselves, I don't think he *really* ever
existed."   That was Italian-like, and so droll.   Some
way I liked Mr. Monti better.

After dinner, the subject of bric-a-brac came up,
and the professor invited us to his son Charles' room
to see some rare objects, and some Japanese paint-

ings.   On the way from the upper landing I stopped
to examine some curious piece of mechanism, which
proved to be the poet's gymnastic apparatus.   He
stepped in to it quite glibly, to show us how it
worked, and stooping over began to raise weights in
either hand with astonishing ease.   I looked on in
amazement.   How strong he was, and after dinner too.

"Come," said he, cheerily, "you try; it's very
simple."

I stepped on to the platform and took up a ring,
struggled tried to lift it up, bent over, tried again;
but in vain; then, oh horror! I heard a fiendish
sound as of stitches giving way; but I would not
give up, so ventured again—this time with a very
red face.   I bravely kept my post until the practiced
acrobat came forward commiseratingly.   He looked
puzzled and said:

" What is it—your muscle?"

" No," I answered faintly, "I think—I know it's
my dress.   You see, Parisian waists are hardly the
thing in which to practice gymnastics, and— "

" Come off directly," said the professor, severely. " Why did you not speak of it before ? " half-relenting. " Let me look." He then turned me around as if I had been a lay figure, and with a grave, serious voice said, in matter-of-fact fashion, " Nothing is spoiled—I never would have forgiven myself had *that* dress suffered." Then he turned the poor offending apparatus nearer the wall, with paramount displeasure. We entered his son's apartment. It was filled with beautiful cabinets in Japanese work, intricate boxes, fans, chains, carved ivory knick-knacks, and screens innumerable, that stood about the place. The doors were paneled with Japanese heads, and some paintings hung upon the walls.

" Look well at them," said the poet clearly, " look well, and tell me what they are."

I saw what they were, but Mr. Longfellow's voice stopped me. Suspecting some trick I refused to answer, and he said with his eyes full of fun :

" No, no, this is not jesting," quite seriously ; " what are they ?"

"Unless my eyes·deceive me," said I, "they are specimens of Japanese oil-painting."

"That's just what they are," said he, composedly. "I thought you could not be mistaken. I was only trying to joke about them, because between ourselves, one can see they are Japanese; but it's very hard," laughingly, "to tell what else they are intended for. My son is fond of this sort of pictures, but to me they look more comical than beautiful. I always want to laugh when I see that moon," pointing to a golden face on the canvas, "it does look so know·ing."

In truth it was a droll painting to look at, but it was in reality too fine a work of art to be so hardly criticised, and good Mr. Monti would not hear of our traducing it farther. After passing a delightful half-hour rummaging about, we left the bric-a-brac chambers. On our way past I spied the now disgraced apparatus. "Do you use it often?" said I to the poet.

"Every morning, regularly," he responded; "it is a splendid exercise, and of positive benefit to the health. I would not miss it." We sat for some time in the beautiful drawing-room, and Mr. Longfellow was very animated and cheerful. He talked on many subjects and delightfully of Italy.

"Ah!" he repeated, "I do want to see it so much. I tell you, every one likes France, but we all *love* Italy."

"This is the twenty-fifth Christmas dinner that we have eaten together," chimed in Mr. Monti, "and I think we *always* have some little word to say for my country. Mr. Longfellow spoils me."

"Not at all," interrupted the poet. "I speak only what comes from my heart."

Signor Monti is amiable, charming, and deeply attached to Mr. Longfellow. "Attached" is scarcely the word. He adores him, and their friendship of many years is another beautiful sentiment, bearing flowers that blossom anew with every spring-time. Besides Mr. Monti's manners, he is a scholar, a linguist, and a man of great talent. He has much heart and is capable of deep feeling, and in many ways is exactly suited to the companionship of a nature like Longfellow's.

On our way home, Mr. Monti did nothing but talk of him and his rare quality.

" He is a man in a million," he would say, " and when you have known him during thirty years, as I have, you will appreciate what a great nature he has. He never changes, and every time that I have seen him during all these years, I greet him each day with equal pleasure, and say adieu with new feelings of regret. He is a great man. There is only one Longfellow in all this world."

CHAPTER XVII.

THE FRIEND OF HIS YOUTH.

"I remember the gleams and glooms, that dart
 Across the school boy's brain;
 The song and the silence in the heart
 That in part are prophesies, and in part
 Are longings wild and vain.
 And the voice of that fitful song
 Sings on and is never still,
 A boy's will is the wind's will,
 And the thoughts of youth are long, long thoughts.'"

My Lost Youth.

"There is no flock, however watched and tended,
 But one dead lamb is there;
 There is no fireside, howsoe'er defended,
 But has one vacant chair."

Resignation.

E determined to go to Cambridge this morning, and once there, were more than repaid for our discomforting drive, by the cordial welcome of the professor. The house looked very stately among the snow-

[221]

capped trees, and the sloping lawn, where the grass
seems in summer-time an unending green, was covered with a thick white pall.   Coming up the front
walk, the poet met us at the door and led the way
into the delightful study.   So bright was the picture
that I could not help exclaiming, " How beautiful are
these walls, the atmosphere breathes rest and comfort."

"And,—" added the professor, "when you come
the many chambers are filled with welcomes."

A   bright-faced   gentleman,   evidently   an invalid, was drawn up before the fire, a little to the
left, I should say, and the professor presented
him as—

"My dear old friend, Mr. Greene."

Mr. Greene has a charming smile, and looked
affectionately at the poet as he said these words.

"Yes," he answered, "your old friend, and now
worse—old and helpless.   You see," he continued,
" I had so severe an attack of rheumatism some time
since, that it has left me in a very lame condition.
I am obliged to sit here in this chair, and cannot

move with ease, otherwise I should get up and make you a profound bow."

"We'll forgive you, Greene," said the professor, cheerfully, "although who can say how much we lose in not witnessing that bow. Perhaps —— suppose you try it?"

The invalid was "not to be coaxed," he said, so we sat down and talked of the weather, Boston, a hundred things, until the poet said,

"I want to show you my Bodoni."

He then led the way into the little room opening out of the study, and brought forth his wondrous treasures. One was a superb volume, and to-day these copies are most rare. Perhaps no one else in America possessed a collection of equal value and beauty. The professor with a scholar's eye, and student's love of ancient lore, fondled it with tender hands. He then went over to Mr. Greene, and together the two companions of childhood pored over a work that still had power to charm.

It was a beautiful sight to witness the tender deference of Mr. Greene towards Longfellow, but

still more touching to see the poet's regard for his
invalid friend. He leaned towards him lovingly,
lifted the volumes with wondrous care, and placed
them in his hands with all solicitude, then took them
away. When one particularly interesting demanded
closer attention, the two old heads almost touched
each other, and the eyes that three-score of years
ago read from the same page at school, to-day
scanned anew, but with deeper love and interest, the
words that they knew by heart, not by habit.

Some time passed; no one spoke, and yet they
read on. Longfellow laid his hand on Mr. Greene's
shoulder, the chair was drawn still closer, and the
poet's silver tresses almost touched his friend's sparse
locks. The faces were different, but a curious study.

The one, bright with a youthful vigor, was
pleasantly flushed with a faint color, and the una-
bated interest that he had in all classic souvenirs
showed itself in the eager look of his eye, and the
ready movement of the outstretched hands. The
supple form bent itself with a grace and facility
that belied his snowy locks and whitened, frost-like

beard. He seemed a man strong not only in intellectual strength, but in a physique that the passing years had in no wise undermined.

But the companion of his youth—how can I best describe him? The head once of shapely grace, and crowned with masses of curling hair, had shrunken with the march of time, and the scanty locks gathered about the still classic profile drooped with timidity and strangeness, as if left alone by their kindred, they abandoned themselves to their fate. The face once the perfection of manly beauty, still retains an expression of great sweetness and refinement. The eyes blue, large, and very bright, smile out with intelligence and genial warmth, and on the broad, high forehead the fine wrinkles are powerless to hide the noble proportions and deeply-marked characteristics of the man's brain and intellectual power. The mouth is a little drawn, but the lips open pleasantly and smile with the slightly conscious expression of one who had been used to fascinate. The whole face is sympathetic, modest and gentle, but—old.

One would think him Longfellow's senior by a great deal, yet the poet first saw the light of day when Mr. Greene's mother was a blushing bride, and many years after his loved friend came into the world.

In youth however, they were fast allies, and M. Greene—whose name I might give in full as George W. Greene—is the grandson of the great General Greene, and has since become widely known as a historian and a very able writer.

The professor looked up as the last page was turned by his friend and said :

" How natural it seems for us to look over these old things once more. Do you remember such, or such a thing (referring to their early life), and how happy it would have made me could I ever even dreamed myself the possessor of such a treasure as this ?"

Greene nodded, and then seeing that we were sitting unoccupied, he said quickly to the professor,

" You know how I love to go over anything with you, but see—your guests must find us strangely oblivious, and we have been neglectful of them for a long time."

I protested, that instead, nothing could have given us greater pleasure than to listen to their remarks, and the talk on the "Bodoni" was instructive as well as entertaining. Mr. Greene sat very quietly looking out on the already fading twilight, and the poet, with my husband lit a cigarette and commenced a conversation on Italy and its wondrous wealth of art, and artistic souvenirs; with reference to different countries he said :

"We all like France, but we *love* Italy. My many visits to 'The Eternal City' never sufficed for all that I wished to learn, and each time seemed more incomplete. Rome is inexhaustible in all that appeals to the mind of the student, and the sight of her seven hills as I came into the city used to make my heart throb with strange feelings of awe and pleasure. I hope to return there some day, perhaps soon maybe this coming summer."

We then entered into a general conversation on Italy, and my husband recalled souvenirs of Verona,

one of the most historical and splendid of all her cities.
The professor spoke with beautiful sentiment on the
ancient landmarks, and said :

"That it was peculiarly interesting to lovers of
the antique. The tombs of the Scaligeri, with their
wondrous architecture, the historic church of San
Zeno, and above all, the superb Coliseum or amphi-
theatre that stands up a glory of the past in miracu-
lous preservation, and an honor to the present genera-
tion of Italy. I never tired of Verona," he said.

"And the tomb of Romeo and Juliette?" I interrupted.

"I did not see it," he answered, "although I saw
the old palace near Piazza delle Erbe, with the inscription, ' *Qui erano le case dei Capuletti ed e Mon-
tecchi*' (Here were the houses of the Capulets and
Montagues)."

"I will send you the photograph," said my husband, "it gives a very good idea of the old tomb,
and although the place is somewhat distant from the
so-named ' Palazzo Capuletti,' it is in a pretty spot.
You go under a grapevined trellis, and at the foot of a

fine old garden you turn to the right, where you follow
the walk that leads up to the open door of the tomb or
chapel. Here Juliette is supposed to be buried beside
her Romeo, and numerous inscriptions testify to the
immortal love of these two scions of Veronese nobility,
The top or upper part of the tomb has worn away, and
it now has the appearance of an empty casket. The
form is still perfect ; the arches above the vault are
time-eaten and marked with sure decay. The sides
of the stone bear faint signs of carved memorials, and
some ancient withered wreaths in jetted wire have
hung faithful to their trust, who knows how long?
There are always fresh flowers upon the tomb, and
such numbers of cards of visitors from every clime,
that the place has a strangely alive look."

The professor was deeply interested, and remarked :

" Yes, Shakespeare immortalized two lovers, and
I regret that I did not visit the spot. I will be delighted to have the picture. It is kind in you to
give it me, and I shall always keep it as a souvenir of
a sad but grand old tale."

A lady then came into the study, and the poet introduced Mrs. Greene. She was the wife of the historian, and was so pleasing that one could not help being favorably impressed with her. She cordially extended her hand, at the same time looking me full in the face with clear, frank eyes, and a smiling mouth that made her few words of welcome doubly agreeable. She seemed a woman of straightforward attributes, and infinite sympathy of character and manner. The word " help-meet " came constantly in my mind as I saw her, and watched her loving, wifely attention to her husband, and how she anticipated even his words, when his speech became energetic and commanding. She joined our circle with admirable ease, but before long the announcement of dinner put a temporary veto on our conversation, and all arose to meet later at the hospitable board.

First of all Professor Longfellow thought of his old friend, and he went nimbly up with the ease of five-and-thirty, to offer him his arm. Mr. Greene took it with a friendly smile, and together they started for the dining-room.

I could not help noticing the tenderness with which the poet guided his invalid guest, nor the touching picture they made together as they walked arm-in-arm through the soft harmonious rooms! The warm fire-light and richer glow of the waxen tapers falling on their aged heads, illumined the form of the one, and cast flickering shadows over the countenance of the other.

Time had changed the outer man, but the fast, firm friendship whose bonds were knit in early youth, had gone on through three-score of years, thickening and strengthening, until its ligaments and fibers were cemented together, as are the roots of strong forest trees, that impervious to the shocks of wind, hail rain storm and tempest, only stand more firmly as the centuries go on, immutable as only are immovable things, unchangeable as the great laws of nature, and—a friendship like theirs.

They walked slowly through to the library and hall, and from there to the dining-room. Longfellow, attentive before, was doubly so at table. His watchful eyes never left Mr. Greene's face, and the daintiest morsels, the most savory bits, speedily found their way to his friend's plate, and whether or no, he was bound to make an effort to eat. It was impossible to resist the poet's cheery voice, first remarking this thing, then urging that, all the time keeping up the most positive belief that Mr. Greene must eat well and heartily if he wished to please his family and friends and regain strength. He was unwearying in his attentions, yet they were so delicately tendered, and with such unobtrusive mien, that Mr. Greene could never have thought that he was an invalid. He was merely a dear friend received with open arms, and treated to the best the house afforded, as should be an honored and cherished guest.

It was the first time I had seen Longfellow in this guise, and if pleased before with his rare sweetness and simplicity of manner, I was even more touched to-day to witness this tender regard of an old friend, and the exquisite frankness with which he showed his pleasure in his society. He could not do enough for him, and during the whole evening his face glowed with contentment and real happiness, while his voice rang out with admirable clearness, and his speech held the happy cadences of one who holds sympathetic converse with a congenial companion.

After dinner, we adjourned to the lovely parlor and had coffee. The room was beautifully lit up, and a generous fire of solid wood roared up in the great fire-place, startling the flecks of soot from their crannies, and reflecting a hundred lights on the polished brass andirons, and near the chimney-place on every bright object that timidly dwelt in the vicinity. Long we sat there in light and comfort. The wind howled without, but it could not penetrate within the walls of the good old Craigie mansion.

The professor had drawn Mr. Greene's chair near the fire, and he threw himself in an attitude of supreme grace in a corner of a sofa to the left of the chimney.

There with his head resting on his hand in a favorite position, he sat talking with his friend, and the hum of their voices was a pleasant accompaniment to the charming softness of the apartment, the crackle of the fire, and the distant soughing of the

night wind.   One could easily rest under the spell of
the moment, and **fancy** it all a glowing "tableau
vivant."

The prospect of a long, cold drive into Boston
suddenly dispelled my dreaming, and the **rest of the**
evening held the one disagreeable **fact of** being
obliged to leave so much warmth and comfort, and
go out into the night; a rude awakening after so
delightful a visit.

As we went back into the study before going
away, the professor turned to a superb bust in white
marble that stood on a table in front of a window,
and said patting the cold, glittering stone :

"Did you not recognize it ?   This is my friend
Greene.   Who would think that this seemingly
strong man is intended for the one that we have just
left; and it's his image," said he, going on enthusias-
tically, " it looks just exactly "—a little sadly—" as he
did—then, when this was taken.   Cher Greene,"
said he tenderly.   Then he looked again at the
white marble that gleamed with singular life and
persistent fascination.   It was so fair that in contrast

I thought of " The Raven," and said unconsciously, " Take your form from out my heart, quit the bust above my door."

Longfellow started and looked up quickly.

" Yes," said he, " but the meaning is different— the words in this case should be 'ne'er take your form from out my heart,' and I am not speaking to a raven, but to my dear and time-honored friend. Apropos of ' The Raven,' what a great poem it is, and how sadly realistic. How typical of the life of its unhappy author. I think of it many times, and know it by heart as who does not? but I also think of the great talent lost in the sudden quenching of that young life, and regret the untimely death of Edgar Allan Poe as one must the loss of a real genius to the world of letters. He was a true poet."

The kind word ever on his tongue for a brother writer, as usual in this case was not wanting. We had no more time for talking however, as the night was really wearing away. Saying *au revoir*, we went out, thanking again and again, our amiable host for the delightful evening that we had passed.

Musing once more I looked at the bust and the lines yet again came into my head.

" And the lamp light o'er him streaming, cast his shadow on the floor." There was the room; there was the "cushion's velvet lining;" there were the " volumes quaint and curious," of forgotten lore; there was everything to recall the poem, yet Poe never could have had such a study as that. How rich the imagination must have been, that could paint so exact a picture. Going over it in my mind it seemed a prophecy of that very chamber, and the tragic scene that cast a troubled dream over the life of another poet, who vainly wept his " Lost beloved." I kept saying the lines over to myself, and they saddened me. I remembered the fate of the young wife, and thought how her husband must have said,

"And my soul from out that shadow, shall be lifted—nevermore."

CHAPTER XVIII.

THE LAST BRANCH OF LILACS.

"Through woods and mountain passes
   The winds like anthems roll;
They are chanting solemn masses,
   Singing 'Pray for this poor soul,
      Pray, Pray.'

"And the hooded clouds like friars
   Tell their beads in drops of rain,
And patter their doleful prayers
   But their prayers are all in vain,
      All in vain."
         MIDNIGHT MASS FOR THE DYING YEAR.

"What men call death cannot break off this task which is never ending: consequently no period is set to my being, and I am eternal. I lift my head boldly to the threatening mountain peaks, and to the roaring cataract, and to the storm-cloud, swimming in the fire-sea overhead, and say 'I am eternal and defy your power! Break, break over me! and thou Earth and thou Heaven, mingle in the wild tumult! And ye Elements, foam and rage, and destroy this atom of dust, this body which I call mine! My will alone, with its fixed purpose, shall hover brave and triumphant over the ruins of the universe; for I have comprehended my destiny; and it is more durable than ye! It is eternal, and I who recognize it am eternal."

HYPERION, page 140.

 LOOKED over my journal to-day in a strangely interested fashion. Since commencing it, I have seen the poet a great many times, and all that I have written seems tame compared with his real worth. He has been too ill of late to receive his accustomed visitors. I spent the twenty-eighth of last December at Cambridge by special invitation, and was delighted to find him in looks the negative of ill-health. He had lost his color, but the unusual paleness did not make him appear unwell. I must say that I never have enjoyed a visit so much, and he was so remarkably bright and vivacious. He talked with great animation, and questioned me on my recent visit abroad.

"It is not yet decided," said he, "whether I am to go to Europe this year or not. I would like to ever so much, but I don't know. It is a long way from home; still we shall see."

He then spoke of his recent illness.

" In my life-time," said he, " I never have suffered so much. I had at first (about three months ago) an attack of vertigo, that lasted forty-eight hours, and after that I was kept perfectly quiet in a darkened room. It seemed as if I never would get well, and even now I can only see my friends for a little while; I cannot write; I cannot read, and must avoid the slightest excitement. But you, chere Pandora, how have you ·been? tell me all about yourself."

When I had finished he said,

" What, writing, and about me? Well, I must hear it all ; so let us begin at once."

Then, in spite of my fears that it might tire him, he entered as usual with hearty interest into my work. The morning passed away, and when luncheon time came he said,

" Why, I am really hungry! That is a good sign."

As we sat down to table he added, " This is like old times. I feel so well to-day, and I am going to make tea just as the first time when you came to see me. Alice," turning to his daughter, " see how well I am. It does me good to have company, and I really think that in your anxiety you have made a prisoner of me far too long. I know that as soon as I commence going about and living in the old way, I shall feel far better."

He talked a great deal, and really seemed anything but ill—or I should say, a convalescent. We went over the old study again, and he showed me a quantity of new things, also a splendid painting that was on an easel in the Martha Washington room, and a very large steel engraving of himself, just made.

It was unusually large. He opened the sheet and said,

" You see all this paper—they try to make a big man of me but the head," pointing to it, " the head is rather small," and, with a little laugh, "*very* natural."

How glad I was to see some of his old humor!

He was quite gay and cheerful; he seemed like a school-boy home for his holiday, and spoke of his plans for getting well immediately. The afternoon wore away, and still we lingered.

"You see," said he, turning again to his daughter, "how well I am, and how it brightens me up to see my friends. I think I must protest against doctors and do only what pleases me; then I shall speedily be cured."

At five o'clock we took our leave. The day had been remarkably fine, and the usually cold December sun was setting with some warmth. The professer started to accompany us to the piazza, when he was called back.

"Not without your cloak papa," said Miss Longfellow tenderly; so back he went half fretfully.

"I cannot imagine," said he irritably, "that one could take cold in such a short time; however "— helplessly—" I must do as they say, I suppose."

Then he put on his mantle and came outside. He walked down the step, put us into the carriage, and with a cheerful *au revoir*, we reiterated our

adieux. I promised to come again very soon, and
the last thing I saw as we went down the avenue
was the gleam of his snowy hair, and the supple
grace of his cloaked form, as he leaned against the
doorway. He kissed his hand in courtly adieu and
watched us out of sight, with cavalier-like grace,
raising his hat a second time at the last moment with
a sweet and friendly smile. We were well out of
the grounds when I remembered to have forgotten
something; I wished to return. So we retraced our
steps. The professor had not yet entered the drawing-room, but stood in his antechamber looking at
some piece of statuary.

He started on seeing us but said, "I hope you
have omitted something that will keep you some
time to arrange."

"No," said I, hastily, "only a question." We
then spoke a few words, and I turned to go.

He shook hands with us again, and said, with a
kindly look, "I will not say good-bye—

"' Wenn Menschen auseinander gehen
    So sagen Sie Auf Wiedersehn! Auf Weidersehn!"

Then we really went away. He did not come to the door, because he had not his cloak. I promised myself the honor of soon coming again to see him.

"I wish," said he cheerfully, "that I were well enough to drive out. It seems as if it would do me a world of good, but I dare not try it yet awhile, I suppose," with a little sigh, "I must be patient."

This was the twenty-eighth of December. A multitude of cares have prevented me keeping my promise, but I have been going over my journal thoroughly. With painful exactitude I call to mind my last visit to Cambridge, and the many happy hours that I have spent in the poet's society. When I go again it will be near spring-time, and perhaps as before, I shall carry away a branch from the old lilac-bush. It is nearly time for them; this is the twenty-fourth of March.

I left my writing, but an hour and a-half later thought of returning to it. I had barely seated myself at my table when the bell rang. A few moments later, my husband came to me with a white face. Looking at me sadly, he said,

" Your visit dear, was really the last.   Longfellow is dead."

He died as he always predicted he would—just " in sight of another May."

CHAPTER XIX.

"ULTIMA THULE."

"Lives of great men all remind us
  We can make our lives sublime,
And in dying leave behind us
  Footprints on the sands of time."
                    A PSALM OF LIFE.

"Take them, O Death! and bear away
  Whatever thou canst call thine own!
Thine image stamped upon this clay
  Doth give thee that, but that alone!

Take them, O Grave! and let them lie
  Folded upon thy narrow shelves,
As garments by the soul laid by,
  And precious only to ourselves.

Take them, O great Eternity!
  Our little life is but a gust
That bends the branches of thy tree
  And trails its blossoms in the dust."
                    SUSPIRIA.

HE morning of March twenty-sixth broke
fair and smiling, and the sun shone until
near noon. Then as if in communion
with thousands of saddened hearts, its face
was veiled. At three o'clock the winds rose high
with sobbing eloquence, and stirred the old trees about
Harvard with a desolate rustle. Appleton Chapel
was filled with mournful faces and weeping friends,
called together to pay the last earthly tribute of
homage to the distinguished dead. While their
prayers re-echoed in the holy sanctuary, the family of
the poet, and the relatives and intimate friends, fol-
owed his remains to Mount Auburn Cemetery. As
they left the house the face of nature grew dark, and
the storm-clouds rent their folds. A misty fall of
snow with tenderness, as if heaven were grieving
silently, gently shed its flakes upon the dreary earth.
It was a last virginal tribute from the Nature he so
adored, more appropriate to the life whose purity equal-
ed its own whiteness, than the colored passion-flower
whose proud blossoms decked his last earthly bier.

On a slight elevation, in full view of the Charles

river " that in silence windest," is the family burying ground. There, with the open face of nature, shall the sun at high noon pour her golden rays, and the shades of twilight steal on apace. Homage from the queen of night shall succeed morn's smiles, and in the silent watch her silver beams shall flood his last resting-place with glory. The stars in their azure firmament will nightly shine on their once earthly brother, now immortal with themselves. When the world is hushed to rest, the elements shall guard his tomb keeping a proud and eternal watch. None can dispute their right, none disregard their jealous sway.

Looking once again on his honored grave, I saw in the day's fading dawn two black-robed figures; with trembling hands and tearful eyes, they placed at his head a handful of flowers—white calla lily, and branches of the violet-tinted heliotrope, whose faint odor and dainty bloom he loved so well. Long they stood there, and then their reluctant steps took them further away from the sad spot. The snow-flakes wildly struggling, tore through the air as the wind increased in violence, and with nature's agonizing mournings, those who loved him best, yielded their long, last farewell.

> " So, when a great man dies,
>   For years beyond our ken,
>   The light he leaves behind him lies
>   Upon the paths of men."

THE END.

1882. **1882.**

G. W. CARLETON & CO.

NEW BOOKS

AND NEW EDITIONS,

RECENTLY ISSUED BY

G. W. CARLETON & Co.. Publishers,

Madison Square, New York.

The Publishers, on receipt of price, send any book on this Catalogue by mail, *postage free.*

All handsomely bound in cloth, with gilt backs suitable for libraries.

Mary J. Holmes' Works.

Tempest and Sunshine	$1 50	Darkness and Daylight	$1 50
English Orphans	1 50	Hugh Worthington	1 50
Homestead on the Hillside	1 50	Cameron Pride	1 50
'Lena Rivers	1 50	Rose Mather	1 50
Meadow Brook	1 50	Ethelyn's Mistake	1 50
Dora Deane	1 50	Millbank	1 50
Cousin Maude	1 50	Edna Browning	1 50
Marian Grey	1 50	West Lawn	1 50
Edith Lyle	1 50	Mildred	1 50
Daisy Thornton	1 50	Forrest House	1 50
Chateau D'Or....(New)	1 50	Madeline......(New)	1 50

Marion Harland's Works.

Alone	$1 50	Sunnybank	$1 50
Hidden Path	1 50	Husbands and Homes	1 50
Moss Side	1 50	Ruby's Husband	1 50
Nemesis	1 50	Phemie's Temptation	1 50
Miriam	1 50	The Empty Heart	1 50
At Last	1 50	Jessamine	1 30
Helen Gardner	1 50	From My Youth Up	1 50
True as Steel....(New)	1 50	My Little Love	1 50

Charles Dickens—15 Vols.—"Carleton's Edition."

Pickwick, and Catalogue	$1 50	David Copperfield	$1 50
Dombey and Son	1 50	Nicholas Nickleby	1 50
Bleak House	1 50	Little Dorrit	1 50
Martin Chuzzlewit	1 50	Our Mutual Friend	1 50
Barnaby Rudge—Edwin Drood	1 50	Curiosity Shop—Miscellaneous	1 50
Child's England—Miscellaneous	1 50	Sketches by Boz—Hard Times	1 50
Christmas Books—Two Cities	1 50	Great Expectations—Italy	1 50
		Oliver Twist—Uncommercial	1 50

Sets of Dickens' Complete Works, in 15 vols.—[elegant half calf bindings]... 50 00

Augusta J. Evans' Novels.

Beulah	$1 75	St. Elmo	$2 00
Macaria	1 75	Vashti	2 00
Inez	1 75	Infelice......(New)	2 00

May Agnes Fleming's Novels.

Guy Earlscourt's Wife	$1 50	A Wonderful Woman	$1 50
A Terrible Secret	1 50	A Mad Marriage	1 50
Norine's Revenge	1 50	One Night's Mystery	1 50
Silent and True	1 50	Kate Danton	1 50
Heir of Charlton	1 50	Carried by Storm	1 50
Lost for a Woman—New	1 50	A Wife's Tragedy ... (New)	1 50

The Game of Whist.

Pole on Whist—The English standard work. With the "Portland Rules.", ...   75

Miriam Coles Harris.

Rutledge	$1 50	The Sutherlands	$1 50
Frank Warrington	1 50	St. Philips	1 50
Louie's Last Term, St. Mary's.	1 50	Round Hearts for Children	1 50
A Perfect Adonis	1 50	Richard Vandermarck	1 50
Missy—New	1 50	Happy-Go-Lucky.. .(New)	1 50

Mrs. Hill's Cook Book.

Mrs. A. P. Hill's New Southern Cookery Book, and domestic receipts..... $2 00

Julie P. Smith's Novels.

Widow Goldsmith's Daughter,	$1 50	The Widower	$1 50
Chris and Otho	1 50	The Married Belle	1 50
Ten Old Maids	1 50	Courting and Farming	1 50
His Young Wife	1 50	Kiss and be Friends	1 50
Lucy—New	1 50		

Victor Hugo.

Les Miserables—Translated from the French. The only complete edition...... $1 50

Captain Mayne Reid.

The Scalp Hunters	$1 50	The White Chief	$1 50
The Rifle Rangers	1 50	The Tiger Hunter	1 50
The War Trail	1 50	The Hunter's Feast	1 50
The Wood Rangers	1 50	Wild Life	1 50
The Wild Huntress	1 50	Osceola, the Seminole	1 50

A. S. Roe's Select Stories.

True to the Last	$1 50	A Long Look Ahead	$1 50
The Star and the Cloud	1 50	I've Been Thinking	1 50
How Could He Help it ?	1 50	To Love and to be Loved	1 50

Charles Dickens.

Child's History of England—Carleton's New "School Edition," Illustrated. $1 00

Hand-Books of Society.

The Habits of Good Society—The nice points of taste and good manners...... $1 00
The Art of Conversation—for those who wish to be agreeable talkers 1 00
The Arts of Writing, Reading and Speaking—For Self-Improvement......... 1 00
New Diamond Edition—Elegantly bound, 3 volumes in a box.................. 3 00

Carleton's Popular Quotations.

Carleton's New Hand-Book—Familiar Quotations, with their Authorship..... $1 50

Famous Books—Carleton's Edition.

Arabian Nights—Illustrations	$1 00	Don Quixote—Dore Illustrations	$1 00
Robinson Crusoe—Griset, do.	1 00	Swiss Family Robinson. do.	1 00

Josh Billings.

His Complete Writings—With Biography, Steel Portrait. and 100 Illustrations. $2 50
Old Probability—Ten Comic Alminax, 1870 to 1879. Bound in one volume..... 1 50

Allan Pinkerton.

Model Town and Detectives	$1 50	Spiritualists and Detectives	$1 50
Strikers, Communists, etc	1 50	Mollie Maguires and Detectives	1 50
Criminal Reminiscences, etc.	1 50	Mississippi Outlaws, etc	1 50
Gypsies and Detectives	1 50	Bucholz and Detectives	1 50
A New Book	1 50	R. R. Forger and Detectives	1 50

Celia E. Gardner's Novels.

Stolen Waters. (In verse)	$1 50	Tested	$1 50
Broken Dreams. (In verse)	1 50	Rich Medway's Two Loves	1 50
Compensation. (In verse)	1 50	A Woman's Wiles	1 50
Terrace Roses	1 50	A Twisted Skein.,.(In verse)	1 50

"New York Weekly" Series.

Thrown on the World	$1 50	Brownie's Triumph	$1 50
A Bitter Atonement	1 50	The Forsaken Bride	1 50
Love Works Wonders	1 50	His Other Wife	1 50
Evelyn's Folly	1 50	Nick Whiffles	1 50
Lady Damer's Secret	1 50	Lady Leonore	1 50
A Woman's Temptation	1 50	The Grinder Papers	1 50
Repented at Leisure	1 50	Faithful Margaret	1 50
Between Two Loves	1 50	Curse of Everleigh	1 50
Peerless Cathleen	1 50		

Artemas Ward.

Complete Comic Writings—With Biography, Portrait, and 50 illustrations.....$1 50

Charles Dickens.

Dickens' Parlor Table Album of Illustrations—with descriptive text......$2 50

M. M. Pomeroy ("Brick").

Sense. A serious book	$1 50	Nonsense. (A comic book)	$1 50
Gold Dust. Do.	1 50	Brick-dust. Do.	1 50
Our Saturday Nights	1 50	Home Harmonies	1 50

Ernest Renan's French Works.

The Life of Jesus. Translated	$1 75	The Life of St. Paul. Translated	$1 75
Lives of the Apostles. Do.	1 75	The Bible in India—By Jacolliot	2 00

G. W. Carleton.

Our Artist in Cuba, Peru, Spain, and Algiers—150 Caricatures of travel......$1 00

Miscellaneous Publications.

The Children's Fairy Geography—With hundreds of beautiful illustrations....$2 50
Hawk-eyes—A comic book by "The Burlington Hawkeye Man." Illustrated.... 1 50
Among the Thorns—A new novel by Mrs. Mary Lowe Dickinson........... 1 50
Our Daughters—A talk with mothers, by Marion Harland, author of "Alone,".. 50
Redbirds Christmas Story—An illustrated Juvenile. By Mary J. Holmes 50
Carleton's Popular Readings—Edited by Mrs. Anna Randall-Diehl.... 1 50
The Culprit Fay—Joseph Rodman Drake's Poem. With 100 illustrations...... 2 00
L'Assommoir—English Translation from Zola's famous French novel........... 1 00
Parlor Amusements—Games, Tricks, and Home Amusements, by F. Bellew... 1 00
Love [L'Amour]—Translation from Michelet's famous French work........... 1 50
Woman [La Femme]. Do. Do. Do. 1 50
Verdant Green—A racy English college Story. With 200 comic illustrations... 1 00
Solid for Mulhooly—The Sharpest Political Satire of the Day.. .... 1 00
A Northern Governess at the Sunny South—By Professor J. H. Ingraham.. 1 50
Laus Veneris, and other Poems—By Algernon Charles Swinburne........ 1 50
Birds of a Feather Flock Together—By Edward A. Sothern, the actor..... 1 00
Beatrice Cenci—from the Italian novel, with Guido's celebrated portrait..... 1 50
Morning Glories—A charming collection of Children's stories. By Louisa Alcott. 1 00
Some Women of To-day—A novel by Mrs. Dr. Wm. H. White............. 1 50
From New York to San Francisco—By Mrs. Frank Leslie. Illustrated.... 1 50
Why Wife and I Quarreled—A Poem by author "Betsey and I are out.".... 1 00
West India Pickles—A yacht Cruise in the Tropics. By W. P. Talboys...... 1 00
Threading My Way—The Autobiograpy of Robert Dale Owen............ 1 50
Debatable Land between this World and Next—Robert Dale Owen. 2 00
Lights and Shadows of Spiritualism—By D. D. Home, the Medium......... 2 00
Yachtman's Primer—Instructions for Amateur Sailors. By Warren........ 50
The Fall of Man—A Darwinian Satire, by author of "New Gospel of Peace."... 50
The Chronicles of Gotham—A New York Satire. Do. Do. ... 25
Tales from the Operas—A collection of stories based upon the Opera plots..... 1 00
Ladies and Gentlemen's Etiquette Book of the best Fashionable Society. .. 1 00
Self Culture in Conversation, Letter-Writing, and Oratory........ ..... 1 00
Love and Marriage—A book for young people. By Frederick Saunders....... 1 00
Under the Rose—A Capital book, by the author of "East Lynne,"........ 1 00
So Dear a Dream—A novel by Miss Grant, author of "The Sun Maid"........ 1 00
Give me thine Heart—A Capital new Love Story by Roe............... 1 00
Meeting Her Fate—A charming novel by the author of "Aurora Floyd"....... 1 00
The New York Cook-Book—Book of Domestic Receipts. By Mrs. Astor.... 1 00

Miscellaneous Works.

Dawn to Noon—By Violet Fane..$1 50		Victor Hugo—Autobiography $1 50		
Constance's Fate. Do. .. 1 50		Orpheus C. Kerr—4 vols. in one.. 2 00		
How to Win in Wall Street 1 00		Fanny Fern Memorials 2 00		
Poems—By Mrs. Bloomfield Moore. 1 50		Parodies—C. H. Webb (John Paul). 1 50		
A Bad Boy's First Reader...... 10		My Vacation— Do. Do. 1 50		
John Swinton's Travels 25		Sandwiches—Artemus Ward...... 25		
Sarah Bernhardt—Her Life....... 25		Watchman of the Night... ... 1 50		
Arctic Travel—Isaac I. Hayes.... 1 50		Nonsense Rhymes—W. H. Beckett 1 00		
College Tramps—F. A. Stokes.... 1 50		Lord Bateman—Cruikshank's Ill.. 25		
H. M. S. Pinafore—The Play..... 10		Northern Ballads—E. L. Anderson 1 00		
A Steamer Book—W. T. Helmuth. 1 00		Beldazzle Bachelor Poems....... 1 00		
Lion Jack—By P. T. Barnum..... 1 50		Me—Mrs. Spencer W. Coe...... 50		
Jack in the Jungle. Do. 1 50		Little Guzzy—John Habberton.... 1 00		
Gospels in Poetry—E. H. Kimball. 1 50		Offenbach in America........... 1 50		
Southern Woman Story—Pember 75		About Lawyers—Jefferson.... ... 1 50		
Madame Le Vert's—Souvenirs ... 2 00		About Doctors— Do. 1 50		
He and I—Sarah B. Stebbins...... 50		Widow Spriggins—Widow Bedott. 1 50		
Annals of a Baby. Do. 50		How to Make Money—Davies.... 1 50		

Miscellaneous Novels.

Sub Rosa—Chas. T. Murray......$1 50	All For Her—A Tale of New York..$1 00	
Hilda and I—E. Bedell Benjamin. 1 50	All For Him—By All For Her...... 1 00	
Madame—Frank Lee Benedict..... 1 50	For Each Other. Do. 1 00	
Hammer and Anvil. Do. .. 1 50	Peccavi—Emma Wencler......... 1 50	
Her Friend Lawrence. Do. 1 50	Conquered—By a New Author..... 1 50	
A College Widow—C. H. Seymour 1 50	Janet—An English novel.......... 1 50	
Shiftless Folks—Fannie Smith.... 1 50	Saint Leger—Richard B. Kimball. 1 75	
Peace Pelican. Do. 1 50	Was He Successful? Do. . 1 75	
Prairie Flower—Emerson Bennett. 1 50	Undercurrents of Wall St. Do. . 1 75	
Rose of Memphis—W. C. Falkner. 1 50	Romance of Student Life. Do. . 1 75	
Price of a Life—R. Forbes Sturgis. 1 50	To-Day. Do. . 1 75	
Hidden Power—T. H. Tibbles.... 1 50	Life in San Domingo. Do. . 1 75	
Two Brides—Bernard O'Reilly ... 1 50	Henry Powers, Banker. Do. . 1 75	
Sorry Her Lot—Miss Grant....... 1 00	Baroness of N. Y.—Joaquin Miller 1 50	
Two of Us—Calista Halsey........ 75	One Fair Woman. Do. 1 50	
Spell-Bound—Alexandre Dumas... 75	Another Man's Wife—Mrs. Hartt 1 50	
Cupid on Crutches—A. B. Wood.. 75	Purple and Fine Linen—Fawcett. 1 50	
Doctor Antonio—G. Ruffini....... 1 50	Pauline's Trial—L. D. Courtney.. 1 50	
Parson Thorne—Buckingham..... 1 50	The Forgiving Kiss—M. Loth..... 1 75	
Marston Hall—L. Ella Byrd...... 1 50	Flirtation—A West Point novel.... 1 00	
Ange—Florence Marryatt........... 1 00	Loyal into Death.... .... 1 50	
Errors—Ruth Carter.......... ... 1 50	That Awful Boy............... 50	
Heart's Delight—Mrs. Alderdice.. 1 50	That Bridget of Ours.......... ... 50	
Unmistakable Flirtation—Garner 75	Bitterwood—By M. A. Green..... 1 50	
Wild Oats—Florence Marryatt..... 1 50	Phemie Frost—Ann S. Stephens.. 1 50	
Widow Cherry—B. L. Farjeon.... 75	Charette—An American novel...... 1 50	
Solomon Isaacs. Do. 50	Fairfax—John Esten Cooke........ 1 50	
Led Astray—Octave Feuillet..... 1 50	Hilt to Hilt. Do. 1 50	
She Loved Him Madly—Borys... 1 50	Out of the Foam. Do. 1 50	
Thick and Thin—Mery............ 1 50	Hammer and Rapier. Do. 1 50	
So Fair yet False—Chavette..... 1 50	Warwick—By M. T. Walworth.... 1 75	
A Fatal Passion—C. Bernard..... 1 50	Lulu. Do. 1 75	
Woman in the Case—B. Turner... 1 50	Hotspur. Do. 1 75	
Marguerite's Journal—For Girls.. 1 50	Stormcliff. Do. 1 75	
Edith Murray—Joanna Mathews.. 1 00	Delaplaine. Do. 1 75	
Doctor Mortimer—Fannie Bean... 1 50	Beverly. Do. 1 75	
Outwitted at Last—S. A. Gardner 1 50	Kenneth—Sallie A. Brock.......... 1 75	
Vesta Vane—L. King, R.......... 1 50	Heart Hungry—Westmoreland.... 1 50	
Louise and I—C. R. Dodge...... 1 50	Clifford Troupe— Do, 1 50	
My Queen—By Sandette.......... 1 50	Silcott Mill—Maria D. Deslonde.. 1 50	
Fallen among Thieves—Rayne... 1 50	John Maribel. Do. .. 1 50	
San Miniato—Mrs. Hamilton.. .... 1 00	Love's Vengeance................. 75	

www.ingramcontent.com/pod-product-compliance
Lightning Source LLC
Chambersburg PA
CBHW030809020726
47499CB00006B/1833